Carver

By T.L. Cumm

Prologue

The sound of high pitched screams filled the air as the woman desperately tried to find somewhere to hide from her attacker. Her silver halterneck top was torn from the neck down. Her curled ebony hair stuck up in all directions as she fled. Tears streaked the panic-stricken face, sending her mascara in trails down her cheeks. The heel of her shoe snapped, sending her hurtling onto the concrete floor. Her knees connected with the ground first, ripping more holes in her fishnet tights. The woman crawled up the steps to the Brooklyn Botanic Gardens in a hope to encounter the security guard, however the guard was nowhere to be seen and she could not hear his footsteps. She screamed as a gloved hand grabbed her hair and dragged her inside. She was abruptly thrown onto her back. She was unable to make out any features of her attacker in the pitch dark. With one quick motion, the knife was slashed across the woman's throat, the tip of the blade glinting in the moonlight. Her eyes widened in horror as her hands came up to her neck in an effort to stem the waves of blood spilling between her fingers. She gurgled as blood surged over her lips with each dying breath. Her attacker simply chuckled as he turned and stalked away, leaving the woman to collapse into the crimson pool that had formed underneath her.

Chapter One- Waking the Demon

The shrill sound of ringing echoed around the bedroom. Aubergine coloured curtains blew inwards from the open windows above the double bed. One would be forgiven for thinking that the room was empty, if it was not for the mound in the bed that was breathing deeply and quietly. The room was still in darkness, the only visible light was coming from the digital alarm clock on the wooden bedside cabinet that read 03:09 am. The ringing continued, eliciting a groan of exasperation from the mound in the bed. A slender hand appeared from under the duvet that matched the curtains and felt around nearby to put an end to the shrieking. It took many attempts for the hand to find the offending object, including knocking various items off the bedside cabinet onto the hardwood floor. Sarah squinted at the brightness of her phone screen as she swiped to answer. She pressed the phone to her ear and tried to stifle a yawn.

"Carver", she responded gruffly, rubbing her palm over her eyes.

"Sorry, boss. There's been a body found at the Brooklyn Botanic Gardens. Suspected homicide," came the anxious male voice on the other end of the phone. Waking up Supervisory Special Agent Sarah Carver was always a fate worse than death and everyone at the Brooklyn FBI Field Office always drew straws as to who would have to complete the deadly deed.

"Give me half an hour," responded Sarah with a sigh as she hung up, ignoring the agent that quickly tried to say goodbye. Her arm dropped down onto the mattress with a thud. Sarah lay in her bed, staring up at the darker than dark ceiling, debating her life choices in that moment, and when murderers will let her get some god damned sleep.

Sarah twisted her body and reached over to her cabinet. She fumbled around for the switch for the small lamp that was situated just slightly to the rear. With a click, the lamp blinked on, casting a warm white glow around the room. Sarah threw back her duvet and swung her long lithe legs over the side. She glanced wearily at the cigarette in the ashtray that had burnt out halfway down and the unfinished glass of Scotch whiskey. Her head pounded with each heartbeat, pressure forming behind her eyes. Sarah ruffled her long red hair that hung down over her shoulders in messy waves as she slid open the drawer to her bedside cabinet and fished out a strip of Tylenol. She pressed two tablets out of the foil strip onto the top of the cabinet with a clatter and then threw the strip back into the drawer, slamming it shut. She carefully picked up the tablets and dropped them into the palm of her hand. She hastily threw them into her mouth and took a swig of the whiskey to wash them down. Sarah slid herself to her feet, the wood flooring cold against her bare soles. With her left palm pressed to her left eye to attempt to stem the blossoming pain, she made her way into her en suite bathroom. She turned on the water to heat up and dropped herself onto the toilet with a groan. She gently massaged her temples, her eyes pressed tightly shut to block out the light. The sound of the water crashing into the basin seemed amplified by the headache. Sarah shed her pyjama shorts and thin strapped vest and stepped into the shower, pulling the navy blue curtain around herself.

Once she had scrubbed every inch of her pale skin, Sarah slid open the curtain and dragged a towel from the nearby rail into the cubicle with her, wrapping it around her torso. She slowly edged her way out, taking care not to slip on the tiled floor. She approached the sink and leaned against the cold ceramic. The mirror over her medicine cabinet which was fixed to the pastel blue wall directly in front of her had steamed up with condensation from the shower. Sarah wiped away a patch from the mirror, a distorted reflection staring back at her. Her hair, now dripping wet, hung over her shoulders and ran down into the towel. Her piercing green eyes were swallowed by dark shadows and her deep red eyebrows that matched her hair were knitted in a permanent frown. She turned on the cold water faucet and retrieved her blue toothbrush from the holder on the back of the basin. She briefly ran the toothbrush under the tap before turning the water off and squeezing some none-branded toothpaste onto it. After cleaning her teeth and spitting out the remnants of the foam from her mouth into the sink, she dropped her toothbrush back into the holder and grabbed another towel and wrapped it around her hair.

Sarah returned to her bedroom with the towels still wrapped around her. She glanced around at her bedroom floor which was littered with dirty clothing that had missed the laundry bag, as well as items that had scattered from her bedside cabinet, namely framed photographs. One photograph showed a smiling Sarah with a handsome young man with curly blonde hair in front of a sunset. The other showed an Alsatian dog. Sarah crouched down and picked the photographs up. She stared at them sadly before setting them back down on the cabinet. She moved over to the large wooden chest of drawers that was near the doorway to the bathroom. She opened the top drawer, fishing out the first pair of briefs she could find and wriggling herself into them under the towel. Moving onto the next drawer, she grabbed the first bra she could find. Casting the towel to the floor that had been wrapped around her torso, she wrenched the sports bra over her head and down until it covered her breasts. She turned to her closet and threw the doors open with a sigh, realizing that she desperately needed to get a handle on her laundry when the case was over. She selected a black blouse with matching dress trousers and blazer. Sarah slung them onto her unmade bed and slammed the doors shut. She turned, ruffling her hair with the towel and stepped closer to her bed. She threw herself down on the bed and grabbed the trousers. Lifting one leg at a time, she wrestled them on and fastened them at the waist. Her eyes scanned the floor for her belt which was just visible under her violet shirt from the day before. Not bothering to get up, Sarah used her foot to slide the belt across the floor and pick it up. She threaded it through the loops on her trousers and buckled it. She came to her feet and dressed herself into her blouse, tucking it into her trousers. With a tie from around her right wrist, Sarah scraped her hair back into a messy ponytail, a few strands of soggy hair falling over her face which she pushed back over her ear. She hitched her blazer over her shoulders and hunted through the duvet for the phone that had disturbed her peaceful slumber.

Sarah checked her watch as she made her way from her untidy bedroom into her equally untidy sitting room. Thirty minutes since she had said she would be at the office. She cursed inwardly at herself and at the new case which had awoken her. Sarah threw back her head and closed her eyes in despair at the fact that she would have to endure the generic coffee at the office instead of her own blend coffee as she had no time to make a new batch. She took her federal issue glock from the unit beside the front door to her apartment and attached it to her belt at her right hip, then attached her handcuffs to the back of her belt. She sat down on the brown leather sofa and pulled on a pair of mismatched socks and her black heeled leather boots. She slid her ID badge and FBI issue lanyard from the glass coffee table and slung it around her neck and pocketed her credentials. With another sigh, Sarah moved back to her front door and grabbed her car keys before leaving the apartment, locking the door behind her and making her way down the stairs to her black Suburban that was parked in the lot just outside of her apartment building.

Chapter Two- Patricia

The agents at the Brooklyn Field Office always dreaded the arrival of their chief when she had been summoned out of bed at an ungodly hour. It was something akin to using black magic to summon a demon. The sound of an engine cutting out and a slamming door attracted the attention of Special Agent Luke Morrison who was conversing with a pair of police officers from the Brooklyn Police Department just inside the yellow crime scene tape which cordoned off the entrance to the Brooklyn Botanical Gardens. Luke glanced over his shoulder at the sound and smiled. Luckily, he had prepared for the impending wrath of SSA Sarah Carver. Her legs took her in long strides, her heels clicking against the concrete sidewalk. Luke turned fully and thrust a disposable cup under Sarah's nose. Without a word, Sarah snatched the cup from him and ducked under the crime scene tape. Luke followed her as she climbed the few stone steps up into the attraction. They did not have to walk too far before they were met with the grizzly sight of a woman lying facing up in a thick pool of blood, her wide blue eyes glazed over and staring lifelessly up at the glass ceiling. Sarah took a sip of her coffee, the hot caffeinated goodness sliding down her parched throat. The floodlights used to illuminate the crime scene was an assault on Sarah's eyes, causing her to grimace and pinch the bridge of her nose.

"You okay, Sarah?" came the gravelly voice of Luke. Sarah squinted and glanced at him. Luke was an attractive man, though not in the way that most women would consider attractive. He had shaggy brown hair that hung in waves to his neck and he had stubble over his angled jaw and top lip. He had chiseled cheekbones and deep brown soulful eyes. He was dressed in a white shirt which was open at the collar, with the sleeves rolled to his elbows and a burgundy tie with black dress trousers. His glock hung at his left side.

"Migraine. So what have we got?" asked Sarah as she crouched down to take a closer look at the victim on the ground in front of her. Luke took a notepad out of the back pocket of his trousers and scanned through his notes.

"Patricia Sparks. Prostitute. She was reported missing two days ago by her street partner Desiree after leaving in a car and wasn't seen again. The report of the body came into the PD around an hour ago by the security guard as he was completing his walk around, then we were contacted an hour later. CSU haven't found any fingerprints on the body or on scene."

"And no one was stationed at this door?"

"Nope. The gardens only have one guard on duty overnight and he is required to complete an inspection of all areas of the site every hour."

"So we're potentially looking at a forty-five minute window in which the body was disposed of while the guard was doing his rounds. Has the ME been out yet?"

"Yes, ma'am. They estimated her death to be around two hours ago around the time that the report came in, based on lividity and rigor. They suspect COD to be the slash to her throat, but they will tell us more once they get her back to the morgue and complete an autopsy." Luke pushed the notepad back into his pocket. Sarah straightened up, her knees clicking. She took another sip of coffee, her eyes fixed to the mottled body of Patricia Sparks. She glanced sideways at Luke who was watching her intently, his eyebrows raised and his dark eyes boring holes into her head.

"Let's get back to the field office," grumbled Sarah. She gulped the remaining coffee in her cup and tossed it into the trash can at the door before making her way back down the steps. She fished her pack of cigarettes from her jacket pocket and slid one out. She put it to her lips and pushed the pack back into her pocket before digging out her lighter. With two clicks, a flame bobbed on the lighter. She held it to the end of the cigarette until it glowed red, then shut the lighter off. She took a long draw off the cigarette before she exhaled the blue/gray smoke. She crossed her left arm over her body, her right arm hanging down by her side with the cigarette between her index and second finger.

"Thought you were giving them up?" came Luke's voice from behind as he took the last step and stood to Sarah's right. Sarah quickly looked at him, then back in front of her at the van that had just parked up with ambulance emblazoned across the side.

"Yeah, well. That went tits up then, didn't it?"

"No shit. You sure everything's okay?" Luke moved directly into Sarah's vision, blocking out her sight of the ambulance. Sarah frowned and chewed her lip.

"Sure. Peachy."

"Come on, Sarah. You know you can talk to me, right?" Sarah took another draw on her cigarette as she considered the man before her, "I know it's been six months since Danny, but you need to talk to someone. You need to open up and let people in." Sarah sighed and looked down at the ground before looking back into her fellow agent's eyes.

"Luke, I know you mean well, but I don't want to talk about this right now." Sarah's initial prickly demeanor was now more subdued and solemn. She took one more draw from her cigarette before she dropped it to the floor and stubbed it out with the toe of her boot. She pushed past Luke who simply watched her as she climbed into her car and sped away.

The Brooklyn field office was silent, which was not a surprise considering it was 04.30 in the morning. Sarah slid her ID card through the lock situated to the right of the glass panel door which had the Department of Justice logo across the center of the glass, and punched in the code on the keypad. The door clicked open and Sarah stepped inside. The fluorescent lights felt like yet another assault on her senses. She walked at pace towards her office at the back, just past the bullpen, her heels clicking on the tiled floor. Her name was engraved into a bronze plaque on a wooden door. She opened the door, allowing the light to filter into her office as she leaned over her desk and switched on the dimmed desk lamp. Sarah slumped into the swivel chair behind her desk. Despite her untidy apartment, Sarah's office was obsessively tidy. She had a large stack of case folders in her in tray to her left next to her computer, and a very empty out tray to her right. An award sat just to the left of her out tray, the plaque glinting in the dull light from the desk lamp. A name plaque sat at the front of her desk reading SSA Sarah Carver- Chief, facing towards anyone who entered the small, almost clinical room. A new case file lay central on her desk. It was emblazoned with the FBI logo on the front. Undoubtedly, this was for her newest case- Patricia Sparks.

Sarah threw back her head, her ponytail hanging down the back of her chair as she slowly spun in her chair, her hands folded over her stomach. It was going to be an exceptionally long day. She lifted her head and looked into the bullpen through her still open door, to see Luke entering and taking his seat at his desk. Using her desk to push up, Sarah came to her feet and made her way through the bullpen to the break room. Sarah was grateful that someone had the cognizance to refill the coffee machine. She switched it on and opened the cupboard above her head to retrieve her favorite mug which was an exceptionally large white mug which had measures on one side which started at the top reading 'Do Not Talk Yet', then 'Give Me Five Minutes', then 'You May Speak' and finally 'Refill'. On the other side, it read 'Boss Lady'. Sarah leaned against the bench which was littered in grubby fingerprints and drummed her fingers on the top as she waited. Once the machine finished boiling, filling the room with its aroma, Sarah filled her mug and then added a generous helping of sugar from the labeled tins to the back of the bench. She picked up the mug with both hands and held it to her nose as she closed her eyes and breathed in the heavenly scent. With a sigh, Sarah made her way back to her office with her coffee in her hands. Sarah placed her mug on the desk, an area where the varnish had worn down from all of the times she had previously set her mug down. She leaned back in her chair and briefly considered the case file in front of her before she sat forward again, elbows resting on the desk and opened the file to the initial police report and crime scene photos. She had no doubts that she was going to need a good stiff drink once all of this was over.

Chapter Three- Migraines

Sarah leaned heavily against the wall to the rear of the office, her back pressed against the wall and her booted right foot pressed against the crumbling bricks. She held her blazer tight around her torso with her left hand, her right hand down by her side with a half burned down cigarette between her fingers. She closed her eyes, tilted her head back and exhaled, cigarette smoke leaving her lips in wisps. She had managed to throw together some notes to try and build a picture of the kind of person she was looking for, but was limited by a lack of autopsy report, and she hated to admit it, another body. Sarah drifted away into her thoughts, the crisp air biting at her face. She was startled out of her peaceful bliss by the sound of her phone ringing. Some hot ash landed on her hand as she dropped her cigarette.

"Fuck" she mumbled, shaking out her now stinging hand and fishing her phone out of her pocket, "Carver."

"Agent Carver? It's Dr Coleman. I have completed the autopsy when you're ready." Sarah pressed a fist to her mouth as she tried to stifle a cough.

"Sure. Be right there." Sarah huffed as she ended the call. Her hand was still stinging and now bore a red mark from the cigarette ash. She pushed her phone back into her pocket and kicked away the bucket that she had used to prop open the fire exit door, allowing it to swing shut behind her with a loud thud. Sarah paced through the corridor to return to the bullpen, relishing the darkness from lack of lighting in the ceiling, aside from the green LED of each emergency light indicating the direction of the fire exit. She ignored the eyes of the other agents that had started to filter into the bullpen, heading directly for her office. She needed to tackle her migraine before she visited the bright, cold room that was the morgue. Sarah dropped herself heavily into her chair and yanked her top drawer open. She rummaged around amongst the odd pieces of stationary. Her fingers brushed against the familiar texture of foil. As she retrieved the foil Tylenol strip, she found it was devoid of tablets.

"Ah shit," she cursed, throwing the empty strip haphazardly towards her waste paper bin. The strip narrowly missed Luke who had quietly sidled up to the doorway, his hand poised ready to knock. He watched the strip sail past him and drop to the floor.

"Sarah?" Sarah's head snapped up at the sound of the voice, the piece of hair that she had tucked behind her ear falling over her face, "Still got that migraine?" Sarah sat back in her chair, ignoring her still open drawer and pressed her hands over her eyes.

"Yeah. Just doesn't want to fuck off. "

"How long have you had this one?" Luke tilted his head, his curls brushing the collar of his shirt, his brow furrowed in concern under some stray curls that lay against his forehead.

"Umm..." Sarah knitted her eyebrows together as she tried to push past the pain to focus her mind, "two, three days, maybe? I dunno. It seems never ending."

"Have you seen a doctor?" Sarah shook her head, instantly regretting the motion as it left her feeling like someone had a jackhammer to the left side of her head. She groaned and clasped her head tightly, "Don't you think you should?" Sarah wrenched her eyes open and glared at Luke. Luke held his hands up in surrender, realizing the expression that had spread across his senior's face.

"Let's just get to the ME," grumbled Sarah as she used her desk to push up to her feet. Her exit from her office was blocked by the slim figure of Luke as he put out his arm to stop her, his eyes sparkling with concern and kindness. She glared at him once more before barging past his arm.

The light that poured through the glass in the doors to the morgue was brighter than Sarah had anticipated, despite all the times she had been there previously. She pressed a hand to the glass as she brought her other hand to her stomach, closing her eyes to try and will away the wave of intense nausea that was creeping its way up her gullet. Her head throbbed with each pulse, making her wish her heart would stop if just for a minute to give her some respite. Sweat beaded her brow. A hand gently rested on her back, making her turn her head slightly and use her peripheral vision to see who it was. Luke stood just to her right with a small smile on his face. Sarah straightened and gritted her teeth, bracing herself for the sensory onslaught that she would endure once she entered the sterile room. A sensory onslaught it was indeed. The light from the surgical lamp above the occupied metal table felt like a needle through her eyes. The room was a contradiction of foul, overpowering odors; the smell of bleach mixed with putrid flesh. Sarah pressed her palm to her left eye to stem the pain. Dr Coleman was seated at his desk, scribbling down notes. He glanced up to see the two agents standing just inside the door. His graying hair was combed back away from his face. A bushy mustache adorned his top lip. Dr Coleman came to his feet and shook both agents' hands.

"Agent Carver, Agent Morrison" he greeted. He tugged a pair of nitrile gloves from the box on his desk and wriggled his aging hands into them. He turned on his heel and took the two short steps required to reach the side of the table. Patricia lay flat on her back against the cold metal table, arms at her sides, a white sheet pulled up to just above her breasts. The stitched cuts were just visible above the sheet. Her eyes were closed as if deep in sleep. Her skin was almost translucent with a sickly pallor settled over her now peaceful looking face. Her neck was supported by a small wooden block, allowing her hair to gather underneath her head. Dr Coleman cleared his throat as he stared at the agents, as if waiting for permission to speak. Sarah waved her hand, indicating for him to speak and that she was listening.

"Patricia Sparks. Thirty year old female. COD was exsanguination caused by a cut to the throat, severing the carotid artery and jugular vein. The laceration is smooth. One quick motion from right to left. Likely a butcher's knife or carving knife used. There were some abrasions to both knees which had grit in them indicating that she fell to her knees at some point. "

"Any signs of sexual assault? " asked Luke as he cast a quick eye to his colleague who had visibly paled. Dr Coleman appeared to catch Luke's countenance as his eyes fell upon the red-haired woman who was squinting and trying to shield her eyes from the light whilst simultaneously gripping her stomach. Dr Coleman raised an eyebrow.

"No signs of sexual assault. No ligature marks noted. It appears as though she was chased for a short time before her killer gained on her and slashed her throat. Toxicology screening showed high levels of alcohol in her system, as well as some marijuana. Agent Carver? Are you okay? " Sarah slowly nodded as she tried to meet his eyes.

"Migraine," she managed to press out, biting her lip as another wave of pain and nausea assaulted her body. Dr Coleman nodded.

"Perhaps you should get some rest, agent. "

"He's right, Sarah. You look like shit." Sarah could only groan in response as she turned to make her way out of the room. Luke glanced at Dr Coleman and took a copy of the autopsy report from the medical examiner's hands before turning on a dime and following Sarah out.

Sarah pressed her forehead to the cool glass of the passenger side window to the black federal issue SUV, her eyes closed. She breathed gently as though she was sleeping. Her skin was pale and beaded with sweat. Luke kept stealing glances at her, concerns etched into his face. Luke decided he would drive Sarah home and drop her car off later. The SUV came to a stop with a small screech outside of Sarah's apartment building. Luke turned and gave Sarah's shoulder a gentle shake to gain her attention. Sarah blearily opened her eyes and returned Luke's gaze.

"Come on. You should go inside and get some rest. I'll fetch your car over later. " Sarah barely had the strength or energy to argue and simply took her bunch of keys out of her jacket pocket and unhooked her car key, handing it over with a sigh. Sarah unbuckled her seatbelt and numbly opened the car door. Her legs swung around the side and she slid to her feet. Luke watched as Sarah walked slowly to her apartment block and let herself in before putting the car into reverse and heading back to the office. Sarah sluggishly dragged herself up the stairs, a hand on the cold metal rail.

As she entered her apartment, Sarah was relieved to find all of the curtains closed to her sitting room with only a sliver of daylight showing around the sides. She locked the door behind her and threw the keys onto the unit beside the door. Sarah slumped onto the sofa and unzipped her boots, kicking them off and across the floor with a clatter. She removed her holstered gun from her belt and placed it on the glass coffee table before retrieving her credentials and setting them beside her gun. With a sigh, Sarah lay down on the sofa and rolled onto her side so that she was facing the back cushions. She closed her eyes as she wrapped her arms around her torso.

Sarah was not sure how long she had been asleep but was she awoken by a steady drumming in her skull. She groaned, curling a hand into a fist and pressing it to her forehead. She slowly rolled over onto her back and brought her arm across her eyes. Her hair had partially come loose of her ponytail and was hanging around her face. Sarah moved her arm away from her face and eased herself up into a sitting position. It was dark out, indicating that she had only slept for an hour or two. She tugged the hair elastic out of her hair, allowing her red tresses to tumble over her shoulders. She pulled the hair elastic over her hand to rest around her wrist. Sarah came to her feet and slid her blazer off her shoulders and slung it over the back of the sofa and took off her ID card and threw it to the table. Still half dazed, Sarah made her way into the kitchen, using the moonlight casting through the windows to guide her. She prepared a jug of coffee and set it to boil on the coffee machine before turning back to the sitting room and onwards to her bedroom. Sarah opened her drawers and retrieved an FBI t-shirt and a pair of plaid pyjama bottoms. She quickly changed into them, her blouse and dress trousers in a heap on the floor beside her laundry basket with her other laundry. Sarah gathered up the dirty laundry into the basket and picked it up before padding her way back through the sitting room to the kitchen. A glint caught her eye behind the front door on the mat- her car key. The incessant drilling continued in her head as she returned to the kitchen. The scent of freshly brewed coffee tickled Sarah's nostrils as she set the basket down in front of the washing machine. She stuffed her dirty laundry into the machine and set it off to wash before pouring herself a mug of coffee and adding several teaspoons of sugar. Sarah returned to the sitting room and set her cup down on the table. She dropped onto the sofa and swept her hair away from her face with her hand as she sighed. She hated to admit that Luke was right. She would need to consult a doctor sooner or later. She had suffered with migraines on and off for years but they had grown in frequency and intensity over the past few weeks. Sarah sat back on the sofa and draped her right arm over her stomach and rested her left elbow on her arm. She nibbled her nails as she stared blankly into space.

Chapter Four- Another Day, Another Dollar.

    Sarah had no recollection of falling asleep. She awoke lying on her back on the sofa with her right arm and leg hanging over the side of the cushions. She groaned as she tried to shake the stiffness from her joints. Her migraine, though continued to persist, had dulled a little. Sarah eased herself up into a sitting position and pushed up to her feet. She checked her watch to find that it was 05.00am so she had plenty of time to have a shower and coffee. She padded her way into the kitchen where she set a new pot of coffee to boil and made her way to her en suite to take a quick shower. Once she had sloughed off the previous day, Sarah quickly dried herself off with a towel and dressed in a burgundy v-neck sweater and black dress trousers. As she did with the previous day, she returned to the lounge where she attached her holstered gun to her belt and pocketed her credentials. She made her way back to her bedroom and retrieved her hair dryer from a drawer. She seated herself on her bed to dry her dripping wet hair.

Once she was satisfied that her hair was presentable and dry, Sarah returned to the lounge where she picked up her mug from the night before and carried it into the kitchen. She smiled as she caught the scent of the freshly brewed coffee. She poured herself a new cup and added her usual helping of sugar before turning back to the lounge. She placed the cup in the same place as it was which could be identified by a brown ring on the glass and dropped down onto the sofa. Her hair hung in waves around her face, accentuating her chiseled cheekbones. She picked up her ID card and flipped it over several times as she stared into space. Her mind drifted to Patricia, at how she had been chased down like an animal and then slaughtered with barely a second thought. She grabbed her mug and took a gulp of coffee, relishing the sweet, coffee flavored goodness.

Sarah drummed her fingers rhythmically against the steering wheel of her suburban to the beat of the heavy metal music that was playing through the sound system. The traffic in Brooklyn was busier than expected for the time of morning. Rain pounded against the glass windscreen and against the black body of her car. The clouds hung low and gray in the sky, casting a shadow across the city. As the cars in front of her crawled forward, Sarah found an opening outside of the Starbucks that she frequented when she was not being called to a crime scene in the middle of the night. She maneuvered the car into the opening and turned off the engine, cutting off the music. She glanced through the window for anyone walking past, then carefully opened her car door and swung her legs around and slid off the seat to her feet. The rain immediately lashed against her skin. Sarah pushed the car door shut and locked it before she tightly wrapped her blazer around her and ran into the coffee shop, her heels clicking rapidly against the pavement. Sarah was thankful that the coffee shop was empty. She approached the young blonde haired barista at the counter whose cheeks were tinged pink with the cold.

"Morning, miss. Welcome to Starbucks. How may I help you today?" asked the barista with a warm smile.

"Could I get two double shot caramel macchiato lattes in a large please? They're for Carver." Sarah fished her wallet out of her pocket and handed the barista two notes, "Just keep the change as a tip." The barista's eyes sparkled as she rang the purchase through the till and retrieved two disposable cups from the stack to her left and set about preparing the coffee. Sarah returned the smile and took a seat at a nearby table. She rested her chin on her hand as she gazed thoughtfully out of the window, the scenery distorted by the rain streaking down the glass. Machines hissed and bubbled as they worked. The aroma was heavenly.

"Carver?" Sarah's ears perked up. She turned to see the barista leaning over the counter with a cup in each hand. Sarah stood up and accepted the drinks before turning to face the rain outside, the warmth spreading through her numb fingers.

Sarah approached the doors to the field office and considered them for a moment before glancing back at the cups in her hands. She was suddenly grateful for the small roof above the doors to shelter her from the rain. She set the cups down on the ground and removed her ID card from around her neck before sliding it through the lock and punching in the code. Sarah shoved one foot in the doorway and hooked her lanyard back around her neck and picked up the cups, using her hip and leg to prop the door open. The office was bustling. Agents talked on phones or typed at computers. Luke stood behind his desk flipping through a case file with the phone balanced between his ear and his shoulder, nodding periodically. Sarah edged her way through the bullpen, setting a cup down on Luke's desk. Luke's eyes fell upon the cup before making their way up to the redhead that was heading towards her own office.

Sarah set her cup down on her desk and powered up her computer before dropping into her chair and opening the case file for Patricia Sparks. Her eyes skimmed the copy of the autopsy report. She had only vague memories from her meeting with Dr Coleman the day before courtesy of her migraine. All she was able to deduct from the autopsy report was that it was not sexually motivated. She knew it meant waiting for another body to show up. With a sigh, she turned to her computer and typed in her password. Whilst waiting for it to load, she sipped her coffee. Sarah glanced away from the screen, through her open door to Luke was watching her thoughtfully, the phone still cradled against his ear and the file in his hands. Her eyes moved back to her screen. She opened up her emails and browsed through them. There was nothing of note. With the cup still in her right hand, Sarah picked up her office phone with her left hand. The handset was clasped in her hand, one finger free to type in a number. She brought the phone to her ear, her hair falling down her arm. It rang a few times before an older woman's voice answered.

"Brooklyn View Medical Centre. How can I help?" came the voice on the other end of the call.

"Hi, Miriam. It's Sarah Carver."

"Oh, hello, Sarah. It's been a while. How are you?"

"I've been better. Listen, I need an appointment with Dr Holywell. Do you have anything?" asked Sarah, her voice low so that she could not be overheard.

"Um... I have one this afternoon if that's any good to you?"

"Yeah, that's good with me."

"Can I ask what it's regarding?" Sarah shifted uncomfortably. She always felt uneasy telling an administrator about her problems.

"Persistent migraines. I've been having them constantly for a few weeks."

"Okay. I've popped a note on record for Dr Holywell. We'll see you this afternoon."

"Thanks, bye." Sarah set the phone back down and sipped her coffee. She gazed anxiously at the phone, her chin in her hand. A knock sounded on her door, attracting her attention to the figure in the doorway. Luke leaned against the door frame, file in hand and a smile on his face. He was wearing a pale pink dress shirt with a violet silk tie and smart black trousers. His ID card hung on his belt. His brown curls brushed against the collar of his shirt.

"Everything okay?" he asked, taking Sarah's calm demeanor as an invitation to enter. He pulled out the soft chair on the opposite side of the desk to where Sarah was seated and slowly lowered his tall frame into it.

"Yeah. Just making an appointment to see my doctor."

"How's your migraine today?" Sarah shrugged and took another drink of coffee.

"It's still there. Not quite as intense but still there." Luke shifted in his seat to dig in his right pocket. He produced a slightly battered box of Tylenol and threw them onto the desk in front of Sarah, "Luke, you are an absolute legend!" Luke chuckled as Sarah set about popping two tablets out and shoving them into her mouth.

"Well, I don't know about that but I remembered that you ran out yesterday. So... Patricia Sparks. Any headway on the killer?" Sarah shook her head.

"Afraid not. I'd hoped the autopsy report would have given us more clues but it didn't really tell us anything. Well, other than the fact that there's no sexual motivation."

"Yeah, that's about all I could come up with. Looks like we'll be needing another body before we get any leads." Sarah nodded solemnly. She stole a glance at Luke. His brown eyes, though ringed with dark circles, sparkled. She drank in everything- the sharp curves of his cheekbones, the way his hair lay on his forehead, partially obscuring his eyebrows; the small indentation in his chin, the thin white scars across his left cheekbone and his top lip. He simply smiled at her, lips pressed together and his cheeks dimpling. Sarah quickly snapped herself out of her thoughts. Her heart was racing, thudding against her ribs.

"Sarah, you okay?" Sarah's hands shook as she tried to redirect her attention elsewhere.

"Oh, um... Yeah. I'll let you know if I come up with anything."

"Likewise. Give me a shout if you need anything." Luke came to his feet and turned towards the door. Sarah caught herself staring at his rear, the way his trousers hugged his buttocks and his thin but toned body. Sarah cursed inwardly at herself.

Sarah glanced up at the tall building in front of her. It was a relatively new building with white painted bricks. Brooklyn View Medical Centre was emblazoned above the doors, the chrome lettering flashing in the sunlight. With a sigh, Sarah stepped forward, the automatic glass doors sliding open, allowing her to enter. The foyer looked far from clinical. A potted plant was situated underneath the stairs that led to the other floors. Several plush chairs were dotted around. Two elevators were directly at the rear of the foyer. Sarah approached the desk to her left. An older woman looked at her. A flash of recognition appeared across her lined features.

"Sarah?" asked the woman.

"Yeah, hi. How's it going, Miriam?"

"Oh, fine. Dr Holywell's ready for you. He's on the third floor." Sarah gave Miriam a nod of thanks before pacing over to the elevators. She impatiently and repeatedly pressed the button, waiting for one of the elevators to reach her level. Doors opened to her right and she stepped inside, pressing the polished chrome button for floor three.

As she made her way along the corridor, Sarah's eyes darted from door to door. Despite the Tylenol, the drumming in her head increased in intensity. Her eyes stung from the lights. Dr Holywell's office was situated at the end of what felt like an infinite corridor. Sarah stopped in front of the door and closed her eyes. She curled her fingers into a fist and knocked twice.

"Come in," came the raspy male voice from inside. Sarah slowly opened the door, the lights searing her retinas. She turned her face away and shielded her eyes. A pair of aging hands closed the door and guided her to a seat by her forearms. She felt the cushion of the chair brush against the backs of her knees as she was gently lowered down. Sarah pressed both hands to her head, her hair entwined around her fingers. She gritted her teeth in agony. Dr Holywell seated himself at his desk and watched the woman in front of him with concern in his gray eyes.

"I understand you're having migraines. How long have you had this one?"

"A few weeks," Sarah managed to press out in response.

"Have you noticed any other changes? Any hallucinations? Seizures? Mood changes?" Sarah briefly shook her head, "Do you have sensitivity to light or sound?"

"Both." For all Dr Holywell was speaking in low tones, it felt as though he was screaming in Sarah's ear.

"Nausea?"

"Always." Dr Holywell shifted awkwardly in his seat.

"Now, I'm sorry to ask after Danny, but I have to ask anyway. There's no chance you could be pregnant?" Sarah gave a small sarcastic chuckle in response.

"If I am, it's the second coming of Jesus Christ."

"Any illicit substances?" Sarah snapped her head up and immediately regretted the movement.

"Jesus! I'm an FBI agent! What do you think?" Sarah's shoulders slumped, "I like a drink now and then but that's it." Dr Holywell scribbled on the lined notebook in front of him.

"Sarah? How long have you been slurring your words?" Sarah furrowed her brow in confusion.

"Wha-? I'm not slurring, am I?" Dr Holywell nodded slowly.

"Sarah, do you have any other symptoms right now?"

"No, I- Wait. What's all the coloured lights?" Dr Holywell's hackles raised, his body gripped in concern.

"There's no bright ligh-" Dr Holywell was quickly cut off when Sarah's head dropped back against the back of the chair and her eyes rolled up into her head. Her jaw tensed, mouth gaping. Her fingers spasmed into claws.

Sarah's breath was disjointed and uneven, choking and snorting sounds leaving her throat. Her body twitched. Dr Holywell slammed his palm against the panic button on the wall and grabbed Sarah under the arms, dragging her still twitching form to the floor. A flustered, blonde haired nurse threw open the door, her chest heaving as she panted. Dr Holywell glanced up at her as he rolled the unconscious agent into the recovery position, gently tilting her head back with two fingers under her chin.

"Get an ambulance please, Nancy." The nurse nodded and turned on a dime to run back down the corridor. Dr Holywell glanced between Sarah and his watch as he timed the seizure, the woman in front of him continuing to sporadically jerk.

Sarah's jerking and twitching had begun to subside by the time paramedics arrived a short time later. Her breathing had evened out. She lay perfectly still on her side, her right hand nestled under her left cheek and her right knee bent up to a ninety degree angle. Dr Holywell stepped past Sarah's unconscious form and opened the door to the sound of approaching footsteps and voices. Two paramedics approached the door, one male and one female. The male paramedic was black and had a muscular build. The female was short and Latina. Both wore crisp white uniforms, a radio fastened to their left shoulder. The male paramedic carried a large red bag over his shoulder. The female dragged a stretcher behind her. Both glanced down at the woman at their feet. The male paramedic knelt down next to Sarah and set the bag down next to his knee. He gently shook her shoulder.

"Hello? Can you hear me? My name's Michael and I'm an EMT." He received no response. He turned to Dr Holywell who had seated himself back behind his desk, "What happened, sir?" Dr Holywell briefly removed his spectacles and rubbed his eyes before putting them back on again.

"Her name is Sarah Carver. She's an FBI agent. She came to me with a prolonged migraine lasting a few weeks. Complaints of nausea and sensitivity to light and sound. No reports of hallucinations or any other changes. I did note some slurring of her words prior to the seizure which she was not aware of. No substance misuse. She saw some bright coloured lights just before the seizure."

"What kind of seizure was it?" asked the female paramedic, quickly making notes onto her clipboard.

"Tonic clonic of unknown origin. No known history of epilepsy. The seizure lasted seven minutes." Michael slowly rolled Sarah onto her back. He tugged the pen torch out of his shirt pocket and peeled open each of Sarah's eyelids, shining the beam of bright light into her eyes.

"Pupils equal and reacting. Size three." He pushed the torch back into his pocket and unzipped the bag, emptying the contents all over the doctor's floor. He flicked a switch, turning on the ECG monitor, "Sorry about this, Ms Carver, but I need to cut your sweater." Picking up a pair of curved safety scissors, Michael cut through the sweater from the bottom, past her abdomen and breasts and through the collar. Sarah's sweater fell open at the sides, revealing her toned torso and sports bra. Michael applied electrodes to Sarah's clammy skin over her chest and her ribs, just under her bra. He plugged the coloured wires into the machine. The ECG sprung to life, a green line bleeping steadily across the screen.

"She's in sinus rhythm," said the female paramedic as she wrote down the reading. Michael applied a large black cuff around Sarah's upper left arm.

"BP is low at ninety eight over forty so let's get some fluids going." The female paramedic knelt down opposite Michael and retrieved a tourniquet, cannula and clear dressing from the pile of equipment scattered around them.

"Hi, Sarah. My name's Christina and I'm an EMT. I just need to pop a needle in the back of your hand, okay?" Christina quickly tore open an alcohol wipe and brushed it over the back of Sarah's right hand. While waiting for it to dry, she applied the tourniquet around Sarah's wrist and picked up her hand, bending it slightly at the wrist. She tapped the skin, encouraging the vein to pop up. Once she was satisfied that she had access, Christina opened the cannula and slowly inserted it into the vein. The flashback of blood told her that she was where she needed to be. With a click, she released the tourniquet and applied the dressing to keep the cannula in place. Feeling helpless, Dr Holywell passed Christina a bag of sodium chloride and an IV set from the pile. Christina hooked Sarah up to the fluids and gave the bag a squeeze to force the fluid through. Michael clipped an oxygen saturation monitor to Sarah's finger.

"O2 SATs are low at ninety percent on room air. Let's get her on two liters of oxygen," said Michael. Dr Holywell took the bag of fluids from Christina and held it up, squeezing it periodically. Christina opened a new packet containing a plastic mask and attached it with clear tubing to the oxygen canister under the stretcher. She stretched the green elastic and hooked it around Sarah's head, her red hair trapped underneath. The mask rested over Sarah's nose and mouth, her breath misting the plastic. Michael packed away the equipment, leaving the ECG out. He came to his feet and dragged the stretcher closer. Christina grasped Sarah's ankles and

Michael hooked his arms under Sarah's armpits, grasping his fingers together at her breastbone. Dr Holywell picked up the ECG, holding the wires and tubes out of the way as the two paramedics lifted Sarah's limp form up from the floor and onto the stretcher. They brought the straps across Sarah's chest and legs and buckled them before setting the ECG monitor next to Sarah's legs. Christina accepted the fluids back from Dr Holywell and rested the bag on Sarah's lap. She threw the red bag over her shoulder and the pair wheeled Sarah out of the room and down the corridor.

Chapter Five- Shattered Walls

Luke charged into the emergency department. His eyes scanned the area. The waiting room was buzzing with activity. Children cried and laughed. A man was sitting with a towel pressed to his hand, blood soaking through the checkered material. A teenage girl had her leg propped up on her mother's lap, her foot alarming shades of purple and blue. Luke was in a daze. The sounds, colors and lights blurred into one. He darted for the reception desk just ahead of him. The older woman seated behind the desk had a phone balanced between her shoulder and her ear as she typed. Luke leaned heavily against the desk with his sweaty palms against the wood as he desperately tried to catch his breath. The receptionist held up her index finger to indicate that she would be with him in one minute.

Luke loosened his tie a little more. The receptionist set the phone down and turned to him, weary blue eyes looking back at him.

"How can I help you today, sir?" Luke fished his badge out of his trouser pocket and held it up to her.

"Special Agent Luke Morrison. I'm here regarding Sarah Carver." The receptionist raised an eyebrow as she glanced him up and down. Luke pursed his lips in frustration.

"Are you family?"

"No, she's my boss and friend," Luke considered his words for a moment, unsure of how best to approach the topic, "She doesn't have any family. Her fiancé died six months ago. I got a call from a Dr Holywell to say she had a seizure. Listen to me, I'm the only one she has right now." The receptionist nodded and typed on her keyboard, perfectly manicured nails tapping on the keys. Luke's hair clung to his forehead and neck with sweat.

"She's in room 124, just around the corner." Luke gave a small nod of thanks as he jogged along the corridor. His eyes bounced from door to door, searching desperately for room 124. He stopped in the center of the corridor, breath caught in his throat. It was a sensory overload with the beeping, hissing, crying and moaning, and the flurries of people dashing back and forth. Luke had apparently ran past the room he was looking for when he realized he was outside of room 125. Luke turned and slowly made his way back to the previous room. He stopped directly outside of the door and took a moment to compose himself. Curling his slender fingers around the steel door handle, he pushed the door open. Luke's heart dropped at the sight of Sarah in the hospital bed, her eyes open in small slits, her lips parted slightly. Her red hair spread around her head like a halo on the pillow. He quietly edged into the room and closed the door behind him. Sarah barely acknowledged his presence. Luke slumped into the chair beside her bed and took her right hand into both of his. Her skin was icy to the touch.

"Hi, Sarah. It's me, Luke. Jesus, what the hell happened?" Sarah's eyes moved back and forth, trying to place the voice she could hear. Her glazed eyes fell upon Luke. His hair was wild from running and his cheeks were crimson.

"Luke?" came Sarah's voice. Her usually strong and authoritative voice sounded small and frail. Luke rubbed soothing circles into the back of Sarah's hand.

"Hey. Yeah, it's me. How are you feeling?" Sarah swallowed thickly.

"I don't remember. I was talking to the doctor and then it all goes blank."

"Dr Holywell tells me that you had a seizure. You were fitting for seven minutes." Sarah furrowed her brow, sweat beading her skin.

"I did? I don't remember. Where am I?"

"Brookdale University Hospital. Has anyone been to see you yet? Any idea what caused it?" Sarah closed her eyes and slowly shook her head.

"How's the case going?" asked Sarah, forcing her eyes open again to look at Luke. Luke's mouth bobbed, unsure of what to think or how to respond.

"You're seriously asking about the case?"

"Am I speaking a foreign language?" snapped Sarah. Luke gave a small sigh. Her personality was clearly still intact.

"Nothing new. No new bodies." Something clicked and Sarah sat up in the bed, the blankets falling to her waist. She began to pluck off the electrodes from her chest, sending the ECG machine into a high pitched frenzy. Luke tried to grab at her hands to prevent her, "What the hell are you doing?"

"I need to get out of here."

"Sarah, you need to get to the bottom of this seizure." Sarah glared at him, one hand tucked into the neck of her hospital gown, fingers dancing over an electrode.

"I need to go home. Now." Sarah had a determination and a fire in her still partially glazed eyes that Luke had not seen in some time. Luke sighed and grasped the metal rail on the bed.

"Sarah." Luke squared his jaw and gritted his teeth, knuckles white from the way his hands gripped the cold metal. His eyes were locked with Sarah's in a battle of wills. Luke's mouth straightened into a line, his brows knitted into a frown. Sarah visibly relented, sliding her hand back out of her gown and allowing it to drop onto the blankets. She gave an exhausted sigh and stared down at her hands, at the white band around her wrist. Luke bowed his head and closed his eyes, relief washing over his entire body.

"At least wait until you've had your scans," advised Luke, his head still bowed and his shaggy hair hanging around his face. He slowly opened his eyes to glance at Sarah who had not moved. She slowly nodded in agreement.

Luke stood directly in front of Sarah's front door. It was of a dark coloured wood and the varnish was worn down and dull. The bronze numbers 23 barely shone in the small amount of sunlight that poured through the tiny window at the top of the stairs that were situated directly opposite Sarah's apartment. A sensation of unease settled in the pit of his stomach as he fished the equally dulled key from his trouser pocket. He was not sure where his powers of persuasion had appeared from, but he had somehow managed to convince Sarah to relinquish her apartment key to gather some new clothing for her since medics had cut up the front of her sweater. Anxiously, Luke pushed the key into the lock and turned it. The door freely swung open which took Luke by surprise- he had expected it to be as stiff and worn as the varnish. He stood perfectly still. His eyes scanned the lounge. It was not untidy by any means, but it was a stark comparison to Sarah's freakishly tidy office. Luke gently closed the front door behind him with the tips of his fingers and edged forward. A mug was set on the top of the coffee table. The inside of the mug was ringed with brown from the numerous cups of coffee made in it. He turned his head to look at the sofa. It was clear to him that Sarah had recently slept there by flattened throw cushions that had been used as pillows.

Luke ran his fingers across the top of Sarah's sofa as he made his way into her bedroom, his eyes darting around at his surroundings. He rested his hand on the glock hanging at his hip as he stepped into her bedroom. The duvet was in disarray on the bed. He glanced around for a bag of sorts. Luke turned to the closet and slowly opened the doors. He immediately located a black gym bag on the shelf above the hanging rail. It took very little reaching for his long arms to be able to drag the bag from the shelf. Luke unzipped the bag and set it down at his feet. Sarah had only two hangers of trousers left on the rail and no shirts. Luke presumed that these were in her laundry. He tugged a pair of navy trousers from a hanger and stuffed them into the gym bag. He closed the doors and turned to her chest of drawers. Sliding the first drawer open, he found Sarah's underwear. Luke gulped nervously, horrified by the prospect of digging through his superior's briefs. He quickly grabbed a pair of briefs and a sports bra and stuffed them into the bag. Making his way down the drawers, Luke grabbed clean socks, mismatched as always, and another navy FBI issue t-shirt. He turned back towards the bed. His dark eyes fell upon the dregs in the bottom of the glass on the bedside cabinet and the half burned out cigarette in the ashtray. Luke picked up the glass and brought it up to his nose, the bag tightly gripped in his other hand. He took in a sniff, catching the bitter scent of whiskey. He set the glass back down. Part of Luke felt guilty for the overwhelming curiosity that made him want to look around more, whilst another part of him wanted to run away. His eyes fell upon the photographs. A knot formed in his stomach at the sight of Sarah beaming and her beloved fiancé- he had not seen Sarah smile like that in many months, six to be exact. Luke silently admonished himself for prying into Sarah's personal life and made his way back to the lounge.

Sarah was much more alert and aware when Luke returned to the hospital. She was sitting up on the edge of the bed, her legs dangling over the side and the tips of her toes brushing against the cold linoleum floor. She gripped the frame of the bed tightly as her back arched forward, her red tresses dangling over her shoulders and chest. She had been freed of wires and tubes. At the sound of shuffling at the door, Sarah turned her head to see Luke standing in the doorway, clutching a gym bag as if his entire life depended on it. Luke edged cautiously into the room as if he were about to enter a ring and square off with a caged animal. Instead of pouncing on him, Sarah smiled gratefully at him which took Luke by surprise. Luke slowly handed Sarah the bag which she accepted and rested on the bed beside her.

"Thanks, Luke," said Sarah as she unzipped the bag and began rummaging through her belongings, setting out her fresh clothing neatly on the mattress.

"So, what have they said?" asked Luke, desperately trying to divert his eyes elsewhere as Sarah hooked her fresh briefs and trousers over her feet and pulled them up under the hospital gown. Realizing that Sarah was going to redress while he was present, Luke turned his back to her and focussed his attention to the poster detailing the twelve steps of hand washing.

"Scans have been done but they won't know for sure what it is yet until the neurologist has taken a look," responded Sarah as cast off the hospital gown, allowing it to crumple into a heap at her feet. She tugged her bra on over her head and pulled it down. She glanced over at Luke who was standing facing the wall with his hands in his trouser pockets and his blazer draped over his wrists. She bit her lip in both amusement and attraction. His pose reminded her of a petulant child who had been sent to the corner in punishment. Sarah wriggled herself into her t-shirt.

"I'm decent," she reported, straightening her t-shirt. Luke glanced over his shoulder first, then turned to look at her. Though still looking pale and the dark circles around her eyes looking even darker than before, Sarah appeared relatively well considering.

"How long will that take?" asked Luke as he watched Sarah run her fingers through her hair and scrape it back into a messy ponytail with the elastic hair tie from around her wrist.

"A week or two. There's nothing immediately concerning so they're letting me go with some migraine medication and an appointment to see the neurologist in two weeks time."

"Uh-huh. Should you really be going back to work?" Sarah's demeanor immediately changed and she fired a dangerous glare at Luke. Luke backed away, hands raised in surrender, "I'm just worried for you is all." Sarah sighed, her shoulders slumping.

"I know. I can't step back knowing there's potentially a serial killer out there." Sarah dropped heavily back onto the bed, her mismatched socks in her hands and her eyes fixed to the star pattern on one sock, the geometric pattern on the other. Luke pursed his lips, his eyes twinkling.

"Just promise me you'll tell me when things get too bad and you take a break when you're tired. Talk to me and let me in." Sarah raised her head and looked at Luke and that's when he finally saw the glass walls around her shatter into a million pieces. Tears brimmed on her lower lashes and she desperately tried to swallow the lump in her throat. Cautiously, Luke approached the bed and perched next to her. Sarah made no efforts to distance herself from him. She caught the scent of his musky cologne. Luke reached his left arm around Sarah's shoulders and pulled her in close. Sarah relished the warmth that Luke's body was exuding. It was comforting. Sarah shuffled closer to the soothing embrace and finally allowed herself to weep. To mourn the loss of her beloved, and in fear for her health.

Chapter Six- Coralinne

Heels clicked against the pavement as a lone figure made her way at speed through a quiet street. A discarded soda can tumbled along the sidewalk, guided by the breeze. The woman pulled her leopard print faux fur coat further around herself, her entire body shivering. Coralinne had just departed her friend's party. Although her head felt fuzzy from the few glasses of red wine she had consumed alongside the delicious carbonara that her friend had cooked, Coralinne felt uneasy, like she was being followed. It was dark out and there were no clouds in the sky. The street lamps cast orange pools on the pavement. Coralinne stole a quick glance over her shoulder, hugging her coat around her and tightly grasping the leather strap of her purse. She silently cursed herself at the plastic bag that was floating behind her. She continued forward, picking up speed. She jumped at the sound of a howling cat nearby, hand pressed against her chest. Coralinne stopped and tugged off her heels. She felt a presence behind her. As she slowly turned her head, she found that she was alone. With her heels gathered in one hand, Coralinne straightened and continued on. Stones dug into the soles of her feet but she knew that she stood a better chance of running if she needed to. Coralinne tugged her cell phone out of her purse but found that the battery was dead.

"Shit," she cursed, dropping her phone back into her purse. Suddenly, she was regretting her decision to forgo driving for the sake of a few glasses of wine. Coralinne glanced around in a hope that a cab would be idling nearby but she was very much alone. She did not live too far away, but she felt uneasy.

"Pull yourself together, Corrie," she muttered to herself. She hated feeling so paranoid, but the news of the prostitute who was murdered shook her to the core. She felt the presence again, even closer this time, but nothing was there. As she turned back to continue forward, a black shape appeared before her, blocking her path. Coralinne yelped and brought her hand up to her mouth, dark brown eyes wide with terror. She could not make out any features of the person in front of her, only that it was the shape of a man and that they had a pair of icy blue eyes. There was silence for a moment before the figure slid a knife from the back of their jeans, the blade glinting in the moonlight and simply said,

"Run."

Coralinne wasted no time in darting past the man and fleeing down the street. She glanced over her shoulder to see the man sauntering behind her, knife still in hand. Stones flicked up from her feet. Her heart pounded a hole in her chest and blood rushed through her ears. Her breath caught in her throat. Coralinne was not sure how long she could run for, but prayed to the heavens that her previous cross country running would finally become useful. A stray dog streaked out from a back alley, knocking Coralinne's feet out from underneath her and sending her crashing to the ground. She took the opportunity to look around. The man was nowhere to be seen. Coralinne picked herself back up from the pavement, dusted the dirt from the knees of her jeans and snuck into the same alley that the dog had come from to crouch down behind a large dumpster. She closed her eyes and tried to steady her breathing. Swiftly and silently, a knife came down and sliced deep into her throat. Coralinne's eyes snapped open and widened, her mouth bobbing. Crimson liquid surged over her lips. Dropping her shoes to the ground with a clatter, she brought her hands up to her neck in an effort to stem the bleeding but it continued to trickle between her fingers. The last thing she saw as the dying light of life escaped from her body was those icy blue eyes staring intently at her.

Sarah was seated on the sofa in her lounge, a mug of coffee cradled between her hands and a crochet blanket draped around her shoulders. Her legs were crossed underneath her. It was dark, leaving only streaks of moonlight across her floor. She cast a glance sideways to Luke who was sleeping on the other sofa. He had balled up his blazer and was using it as a pillow. A stray lock of hair hung over his face and nose. His tie hung loosely around his neck and his sleeves were haphazardly rolled to his elbows. His chest gently rose and fell. Sarah could not help but watch him in admiration. Luke had insisted on keeping Sarah company, even if it meant camping out on her sofa. Initially, Sarah felt awkward about having him in her home, but then she remembered that he had been in earlier in the day and that he had had to reluctantly go into her underwear drawer. Her headache had subsided somewhat. Sarah yawned and her eyes began to droop. She set her half drunk coffee on the table and unfurled herself from the sofa. She quietly picked her way to her bedroom and dropped onto the side of her bed. She swung her legs up onto the mattress and tugged the duvet over herself. Sarah lay back into her pillows and sighed in bliss.

The scent of freshly brewed coffee awoke Sarah the following morning. With closed eyes, Sarah poked her nose out from her duvet and sniffed to try and locate the smell, suddenly resembling a mole tunneling its way out of the ground. She cracked open her eyes and peeked over the duvet to find Luke setting a mug down on her bedside cabinet and removing the empty glass. Luke smiled at her and turned away to return to the kitchen. She shoved the duvet away and used her arms to push herself up to a seated position. She reached over and grabbed the mug, the steam still rising from the top of the mug from the coffee inside, and cradled it in her hands, the warmth spreading through her fingers. She could hear the sound of a phone ringing and then Luke chatting in hushed tones. Sarah brought the mug to her lips and sipped her coffee. Luke appeared at the doorway, cell phone in his hand and a grim expression across his exhausted face. He leaned against the door frame. Sarah looked at him, mug still pressed against her bottom lip. She slowly moved the mug away, eyes wide.

"What happened?" asked Sarah. Luke sighed and looked at the floor.

"Another body turned up in an alley just off of Rogers Avenue. Same MO." Sarah quickly set the mug down on the bedside cabinet and threw the duvet back, swinging her legs out of bed and coming to her feet quicker than expected, leaving her with a wave of dizziness. She pressed a palm to her forehead.

"Give me five minutes to change," she ordered, already making her way to her drawers and gathering clean clothing. Luke nodded in response and returned to the lounge. Sarah appeared in the lounge five minutes later and in record time. Luke was in the process of shouldering his blazer. Sarah was dressed in a pair of black jeans and a dark purple t-shirt. Although her ensemble was more casual than usual, Sarah had made an effort to at least resemble being a professional. She hooked her lanyard and ID card around her neck and holstered her glock. Neither of the pair spoke as they filed out of Sarah's apartment.

Rogers Avenue was bustling with early morning commuters and shoppers. A crowd had gathered around an opening to a back alley which had been cordoned off with yellow crime scene tape. A pair of police officers were stationed at the entrance whilst another stood near the dumpster scribbling down notes. Luke's dark blue BMW pulled up to the curb and came to a stop. Sarah was first out of the passenger side, her hand already reaching for her credentials. Luke followed closely behind her, credentials in his hand. They barged through the crowd of onlookers and flashed their badges at the police officers. Luke held the tape up for Sarah to duck underneath, then bent his tall, lanky frame down to do the same. Luke straightened, his knees clicking. He fished through his blazer pockets for some nitrile gloves. He handed a pair to Sarah who looked at them, then at Luke. The gloves were twice the size of Sarah's hands. Sarah chuckled and wriggled her hands into them. Luke blushed as he pulled on his gloves with a snap. Sarah crouched down next to the body. The woman's fur coat was open and hung at either side of her. Her ebony curled hair was matted and caked with congealed blood. The woman's glazed eyes were wide with terror. A neat, deep cut snaked across her throat. Blood was dried to her chin. Her hands hung limply at her sides and were also covered in dried blood.

"Certainly has a type," commented Luke as he crouched down next to Sarah and closely observing the woman's hair, "Likes women with black curly hair."

"Yeah. Look at her knees. They're all grazed like she fell over, just like Patricia Sparks. She's also got stones in her feet like she was walking barefoot."

"Makes sense," replied Luke as he hooked a finger in a shoe and held it up. He glanced out to the busy street, "I wonder if any of these buildings have any security cameras. It's clear that she was killed here but this is just off a busy street so it's more likely that someone had to see something." Sarah grabbed the woman's purse and opened it. She slid the burgundy leather wallet out of the purse and opened it to reveal the woman's driving license.

"Coralinne Smith. She's a Brooklyn native. We'll see what we can find on her when we get back to the office." Sarah turned to the police officer who was listening intently to the pair, "Has the ME been yet?" The officer cleared his throat and twitched his graying mustache. Luke tugged the half battered notebook out of his pocket to make some notes.

"Yes, ma'am. He estimated the time of death to be around eight hours ago based on lividity but will give a more accurate time when he completes the autopsy. He thinks the COD is likely to be blood loss from the cut to the throat." Sarah nodded.

"Who found her?" asked Luke, eyes screwed up in concentration.

"The head chef at the restaurant here came out to discard some unused food and found her and then rang it in. That was around an hour ago. As soon as the call came in, we knew we needed to call you guys."

"Thanks, officer. MO is the same as Patricia so this has to be the same killer. I think that these women are a surrogate for someone. We need to go back and find out if there are any similar cases that might give us some inkling as to what's going on." Luke nodded and stuffed the notebook back into his back pocket. They both came to their feet and removed their gloves before depositing them into a bag being held open by the police officer and making their way back through the crowd of people craning to get a view of the dead body to the car.

Chapter Seven- Memories

Sarah's nose was virtually touching the papers on her desk as she poured over the police report from the latest crime scene. Everything was pointing her in the direction of a sadistic person who enjoys chasing his victims before slashing their throats. A person who was using Caucasian women with black curly hair as surrogates. Yet again, Sarah found herself no further forward. This killer was meticulous, ensuring that he left no trace of evidence on his victims. Sarah lifted her head and peered over the top of her desk, past her name plate to Luke at his desk, whose brow was furrowed in concentration as he stared intently at his computer screen. A pen was clenched between his teeth, partially resting against his bottom lip. His left hand maneuvered the mouse whilst the fingers on the other hand drummed against the desk in frustration. Sarah straightened in her chair and tucked the report back into the manila folder. She pressed her palms to her desk and pushed herself up to her feet. Perhaps Luke would fare better with a second pair of eyes to study the CCTV footage from the shop directly opposite the back alley.

Sarah quietly made her way past the bustling desks in the bullpen. The other agents were heavily wrapped up in other tasks to notice their chief passing by. Sarah slipped into the break room. She was relieved to find the coffee pot refilled. She flicked the switch on the machine to power it on, a red light indicating that it was about to work its magic on the caffeinated goodness. Sarah retrieved her usual mug from the cupboard above her head and a blue FBI issue mug. She gently set them down on the counter. She drummed her fingertips against the counter top as the coffee machine bubbled and hissed to her left. Sarah's eyes stared at the battered cupboard door as her mind drifted.

Sarah lay amongst the sand, eyes closed and sun bleaching down on her pale skin. Her hands were clasped behind her head. A silhouette blocked out her sun, causing her to open one eye and peer questioningly at the cause of the shadow. A handsome man with blonde curly hair that hung over his forehead but neatly trimmed at the back and sides hovered over her, a pearly white smile bearing back at her. He wore a pair of floral beach shorts and his toned muscles rippled. Sarah smiled at him.

"Danny..." she sighed happily. Danny lay down next to her, arm curled around her waist and drawing her in close. His cologne tickled her nostrils. Sarah rested her palm against his angular cheek.

"I love you, Sarah Carver."

"I love you too, Danny Fairfax."

Sarah was abruptly snapped out of her thoughts by the coffee machine giving out its final hiss. A swell of sorrow tightened around her chest. It had been six months. Six months since her beloved was taken away from her. One hundred and eighty two days since the drunk driver took away an innocent life and left Sarah permanently scarred by grief. Survivor's guilt was what the therapist had told her. Guilt. Sarah felt that by the truckload every single damned day. Danny had surprised her at the office with lunch and a bouquet of deep red roses and was on his way home when the truck barrelled through a red light and plowed into the side of his sedan. They had been set to marry in a matter of weeks before that fateful day.

Sarah's features hardened as she poured the steaming coffee into the mugs before setting the coffee pot back into the machine. She added a generous helping of sugar to her own coffee from the tins in front of her, then quietly opened the fridge to retrieve the milk. She poured some milk into her own coffee and returned the carton of milk to its place in the door of the fridge. Sarah rested her palms against the counter and bowed her head. With a sigh, she gathered up a mug into each hand and made her way back to Luke. Another agent was heading in Sarah's general direction, nose buried deep in a manila folder. Luckily, Sarah had the wherewithal to take a side step and dodge the oncoming woman and potential coffee calamity. Sarah sidled up to Luke's desk where he was still deep in concentration at the CCTV footage on his screen. She perched on the edge of the desk and set the mug of coffee down in front of him. Luke's eyes shifted from the screen to the mug, then up to Sarah who was smiling down at him. Despite her smile, there was a sadness lingering there in her green orbs. Luke looked exhausted. He had dark circles around his youthful eyes and the stubble had grown thicker on his chiseled jaw. Sarah grasped her mug between her hands and brought it up to her lips.

"How's it going?" she asked, a smile dancing on her lips. Luke leaned back in his swivel chair and ran his hands through his shaggy hair.

"Nothing from the nail bar and I've barely made a dent in the footage from the convenience store."

"How about we look together?" Sarah had a playful expression on her face. Or was it lust? Luke raised his eyebrows at her and turned back to the screen. He clicked the play button on the video. Sarah shifted herself so that she was positioned behind him, leaning over his shoulder. Luke swallowed, his Adam's apple bobbing. Sarah was close. Very close. Coffee. She smelt of coffee. Sarah could smell his musky cologne. They watched the grainy footage on the screen, eyes darting around at the various people passing the store. Luke knotted his brows in concentration. Sarah's breath hitched in her throat.

"Wait! Rewind it a little." Luke clicked on the arrow to take the video back a few frames, "There! There's our vic." Luke leaned in closer, his tie draped across the keyboard.

"She's running and a dog trips her up," added Luke.

"And then she ducks down behind the dumpster," responded Sarah, pointing her middle finger at the rectangular shape just in shot on the screen.

"This looks like our guy." A figure appeared on screen wearing all black and a ski mask on, "He looks like he could easily be six foot tall and a hundred and eighty pounds."

"Muscular build. He goes into the alley after her and boom." Sarah stood up straight, eyes still fixed to the screen.

"So what does this tell us?" Luke turned in his chair and angled his head up to face Sarah. Sarah glanced down at him, the playful smile still dancing on her lips.

"That he's six foot tall and a hundred and eighty pounds?" Luke pursed his lips and folded his arms across his chest indignantly. Sarah's eyes twinkled as she brought the cup to her lips again and sipped her coffee. The pair stared at one another, eyes locked in a battle of wills. The concentration was broken by the sound of Sarah's cell phone ringing. She fished it out of her pocket, her mug cradled in her other hand, and held it to her ear.

"Carver."

"Good afternoon, Agent Carver. I have completed the autopsy. As with our previous victim, Ms Smith appears to have been chased and fallen as evidenced by the abrasions to her knees. Same MO. Single, clean laceration to the throat severing the carotid and jugular. No ligature marks. Tox screen showed alcohol in her system. Not as high a level as our previous victim but too high for the legal drink-drive limit." The words hit Sarah like a punch in the gut.

"Thanks, doc." Sarah sighed and hung up the call. She pushed her phone back into her jeans pocket. Luke had been watching the exchange and the change in Sarah's demeanor. It was as if the walls were visibly building around her.

"Sarah?" Sarah looked down at Luke, the twinkle gone from her eyes and a stone cold hardness in her features. As quickly as she hardened, Sarah's face softened again. Luke knew immediately that the medical examiner's words had triggered a memory in Sarah, "Sarah? Are you okay?" Sarah nodded morosely and stared into her half cold mug of coffee, "You remember you can talk to me, right?"

"I know. Let's just find this bastard." Luke studied Sarah's face, desperately trying to read her thoughts. His eyes narrowed.

"What are you thinking?"

"Undercover. Set a trap for him. So far he has killed every two days. We have forty eight hours before he kills again." Luke wrinkled his brow in thought, fingers curled under his chin and his elbow resting on his other arm that was draped across his abdomen.

"Who would you assign? None of the other female agents have undercover experience, and they sure as hell don't match his victimology." Sarah's playful smile returned. Luke instantly realized what Sarah was implying, "Sarah! You can't be serious?" Sarah turned and stalked away to her own office, heels clicking on the floor and her hips swaying seductively. Luke pursed his lips in frustration as he watched her disappear into her office.

Chapter Eight- Under the Cover of Darkness

Sarah watched as hues of purple, blue and black swirled around the water and vanished down the plughole as she rinsed the temporary black dye from her hair. Her back ached from kneeling at the basin of her shower. Her usually crimson locks had been dyed a deep shade of black and hung limply over her face, dripping into the basin. Slowly, Sarah came to her feet and hooked the shower head back onto the holder. She quickly turned the chrome knob to turn off the water. The steaming water went from crashing into the basin to a steady dripping. Sarah turned to the sink and wiped away a patch of condensation from the mirror with the palm of her hand. She barely recognised her own reflection as it stared back at her. The dark hollows around her eyes looked even darker and her skin was paler than usual with the black hair that now framed it. The water dripping from the ends of her hair traced with a gray tinge over her pale shoulders. Sarah quickly wrapped a towel around her hair and another around her torso, then padded through to her bedroom. A shopping bag lay haphazardly on her unmade bed. Sarah opened the bag and tugged out the contents, setting them neatly on her bed. She gazed at the clothing which was far from anything she would ever choose for herself- a short, leather look skirt, a slinky black camisole and a leopard print faux fur jacket.

Sarah sighed and sat down on the edge of her bed, taking the black kohl eyeliner, mascara and blood red lipstick into her hands. Make up was never anything she had an interest in, but for one night, it would have to be. She returned to the bathroom and used the mirror on the medicine cabinet to guide her. First, she applied a thick line of eyeliner over her upper eyelid and dragged it out into a flick at the outer corner of her eye, then made a thinner line on the waterline of her lower eyelid. She repeated the action on her other eye, though found this somewhat more difficult. She set the eyeliner down on the back of the basin and picked up the mascara. Sarah quickly swept the brush over her upper and lower lashes. Her eyes suddenly appeared darker and more hollow. She made a mental note to take better care of herself, and maybe use a sunbed every once in a while. She applied lipstick and smacked her lips. Sarah chuckled as she realized that she somewhat resembled her teenage self during her goth phase.

Sarah made her way back to her bedroom, ruffling her hair with the towel. She quickly dressed herself in her underwear, then the uncharacteristic outfit she had bought from a charity store. She took out her hairdryer to blow dry her hair, and then curled it with a curling wand she had acquired from one of the other agents at the field office. She glanced at her clock- Luke would be due to arrive soon.

Luke pulled silently into the parking lot of Sarah's apartment complex and turned off the engine. He watched as a figure descended the stairs and exited the building. The figure approached the car, a faux fur jacket pulled tight around her torso, a pair of pale yet stunning legs carrying her in swift steps. A face appeared at the driver's side window, causing Luke to jump in fright. Sarah grinned at the man clutching his chest as she made her way around to the passenger side. She slid herself into the seat and tugged the door closed. Luke glared at her.

"Jesus, Sarah!" he gasped, resting his head back against the headrest of the seat. Sarah giggled at him. She snatched up the small black case in the center console and popped it open. She took out one of the earpieces and pushed it into her right ear. Luke, having managed to compose himself somewhat, took the other and pushed it into his own ear.

"All good?" asked Sarah. Luke nodded and gave a thumbs up in response. Luke sighed and gripped the steering wheel with both hands, staring out of the windscreen at the swaying trees ahead. Sarah raised an eyebrow, her piercing green eyes boring a hole into his head.

"Luke?"

"Are you sure about this, Sarah? I mean, you're not exactly in the best of health right now and-" Sarah quickly cut him off, her eyes blazing and her lips pursed.

"Luke. No one else is suitable for this. I am. I can do this. Do not underestimate me." Luke swallowed thickly as he turned his head to face the woman sitting next to him.

"Just... Please be careful." Sarah turned to look out of the window. Luke started the engine and pulled out of the parking complex.

Sarah hugged herself as she slowly walked down the street, her heels clicking rhythmically against the sidewalk. She was very much alone. The breeze whipped empty candy wrappers and chip packets around her bare ankles. Her hackles raised at a presence approaching behind her. She tightly gripped the handle of her firearm which was hidden beneath her jacket. She glanced around to find there was no one there. Sarah picked up her pace, heels clicking more frantically. Her hold on her glock tightened, knuckles white. She spotted a back alley nearby. Silently, Sarah slipped into the back alley and hid in the shadows. Heavy footsteps approached and stopped. She held her breath and slid the glock out from under her jacket. As the footsteps moved into the back alley, Sarah swung her arm out and the butt of the gun connected with something fleshy. A grunt followed. Sarah glanced out to see a figure entirely in black clutching his face. Luckily for Sarah, she excelled in the physical aspect of her job. She broke into a run, darting past the figure and made her way down the street. Luke's voice came through her earpiece.

"Sarah! Is everything okay?" asked Luke, a hint of panic in his voice.

"Yeah. He found me though I think I may have broken his nose." She whipped her head around, her hair being carried by the breeze and getting caught on her eyelashes. The man had broken into a run and was following behind, "He's on my tail."

"I haven't got a visual on you or the suspect," responded Luke.

"I'm getting close." Sarah stopped and faced the man who was gaining on her. She pointed her glock at him and fired a single shot. The man sagged to the ground. Luke's voice crackled again over the earpiece.

"Sarah! I heard shots!"

"I'm fine. Suspect is down." Sarah holstered her gun under her jacket and sighed. She moved over to the man and knelt down beside him, taking care to maintain her modesty. She grasped the bottom of the ski mask and tugged it upwards. The man had a track of blood over his lips and chin from a very crooked nose. His blue eyes were surrounded by deep lines. A small patch of dark hair adorned his chin, just under his bottom lip. A dark pink scar snaked over his left eye, coming to rest near the corner of his mouth.

"Caucasian male. Blue eyes. He has a scar over his left eye coming down to his mouth. Black hair. Looks to be in his forties," said Sarah, her eyes fixed to the unconscious man in front of her. Blood was spreading from the hole in his shoulder, across his black sweater. Without warning, a hand shot up and tightly gripped the back of Sarah's hair. She grasped the hand with both of hers to try and dislodge the fingers that were entwined in her curls. The hand dragged her head down until her forehead connected with the pavement. Sarah dropped to the ground, blood running down her nose from an abrasion to her forehead. Her surroundings swam hazily before her eyes. She vaguely heard the sound of running, then Luke appeared over her.

"Sarah! Sarah! Can you hear me?" Sarah wanted to respond but it was as if the messages were not reaching her mouth from her brain. Black spots danced before her eyes, Luke's voice sounding like he was under water. Sarah was unable to stop herself from succumbing to the darkness.

Chapter Nine- Heresy

Sarah sat on the ledge on the back of the ambulance as a paramedic gently dabbed away the congealed blood from her forehead and face. Sarah stared at the backs of her hands. She shivered as a cold wind whipped around her. She could not feel the dull throb from her wounds. What she felt instead was pure boiling rage that their killer had managed to flee. The sounds of stones crunching under boots attracted her attention away from her hands. Her bleary eyes followed the scuffed leather boots, up the black dress trouser legs, the navy button down shirt to Luke's rugged features. His eyebrows were raised in concern. Sarah set her jaw and pursed her lips as she stared back at the ground.

"How badly were you hurt?" asked Luke as he slid his blazer from his shoulders and draped it around Sarah. Her thin frame was lost under the heavy fabric of the jacket. Sarah poked her hands out from under the jacket and pulled it tighter around herself.

"Mild concussion. I'll live. Can't say the same for our suspect though when I get my hands on him again." Luke let out a deflated sigh and rubbed his brow with the pads of his fingertips. The flashing red lights from the ambulance merged with the blue lights from the surrounding police vehicles lit up the otherwise dark buildings around them.

"We'll check nearby emergency rooms for anyone matching the description you gave. You managed to get a shot in so he's wounded." Sarah laughed darkly, her eyes transfixed on a single stone on the road. Luke folded his arms across his chest, his skin bristling with the cold and tapped his foot in annoyance. Sarah's eyes traced across the road to the bobbing boot. A gust of wind blew some of her hair into eyes, black strands clinging to her eyelashes.

"Snap out of it!" yelled Luke in frustration, his usually serene brown eyes blazing with anger. Sarah noted the way he clenched his jaw. It was a side of Luke she had never witnessed and she was not sure how she felt about it. For the first time since their failed attempt at taking down their suspect, Sarah stared into Luke's eyes. There was indeed anger there, though there was also disappointment. She knew deep down that Luke had been right- she was not in the best of health for undercover operations, and they would be more likely to find their suspect given that he would be sure to attend an emergency room with a gunshot wound to his left shoulder but her ego got the better of her. Sarah sighed. She hated being wrong and hated admitting it even more so. Her features softened.

"I'm sorry. You were right, Luke." Luke's foot immediately stopped tapping. His eyebrows shot up and his mouth gaped. It was as though his world had just flipped over. Luke's arms dropped to his sides. He curled his left arm around Sarah's shivering shoulders, drawing her closer to his hip. Sarah nestled into the touch.

"Come on. Let's take you home." Sarah nodded softly as she allowed Luke to ease her into a standing position. His blazer almost reached her knees.

The pair drove in silence. Sarah gazed out of the passenger side window at the trees and buildings zipping past. Their surroundings blurred into a multitude of colors. Periodically, Luke would glance over at her. He had muted the police radio in the center console to allow Sarah some peace and quiet. As they reached the parking lot of Sarah's apartment complex, she turned her head to face Luke. The nearby street lamp cast an eerie orange glow across the side of her face.

"Luke?" Luke turned to face the small voice next to him, his hands still gripping the steering wheel.

"Yeah?"

"Thank you." Luke raised an eyebrow.

"For what?"

"Everything." Luke swallowed thickly. He quickly pulled into a parking space and turned off the engine.

"Let me walk you up." Luke exited the car first, then opened the passenger side door. He extended his hand for Sarah to grab onto. He assisted her out of the car and draped his arm around her shoulders once again to guide her into the complex and up to her apartment. Sarah moved sluggishly, her eyes downcast. At her apartment door, Sarah dropped the cold steel of her door key in Luke's clammy palm. Luke pursed his lips and slid the key into the lock of the door, turning it with a soft click. He guided her gently into the hallway and closed the door behind him, streaks of orange lighting casting a shadow against the back of the front door. The street lamps highlighted the shadows around Luke's eyes and under his sharp cheekbones.

Sarah's hand reached up, her fingertips gently tracing around Luke's eye and over his cheek. Luke's breath hitched in his throat, his brown eyes fixed on Sarah's shadowed form. Her hands came to rest on Luke's chest. Luke felt his heart beating a hole into his ribs. He did not anticipate Sarah forcing him back against the front door. His spine collided with the wood which caused him to grunt in surprise. Sarah wrapped her hands around the back of Luke's neck and entwined her fingers in his hair. He took note of her perfume- it was sweet, yet musky. Sarah pressed herself into Luke's body. He could feel her breasts pressing into his chest. Luke gulped as Sarah dragged Luke's head down so that his lips brushed against hers. His hair tickled her skin. Sarah pulled back slightly, staring intently into Luke's terrified eyes.

"Sarah? I-I-"

"Just shh and kiss me."

"Sarah-" Luke was quickly silenced as Sarah forced her lips against his. His lips were softer than she had expected. Luke squeezed his eyes shut as Sarah's fingers tightened around his hair, her other hand cupping his jaw. Luke tasted of coffee and he smelled strongly of cologne. Sarah tasted of cigarettes and whisky. Luke pulled back, losing himself in Sarah's piercing stare. His chest heaved with each breath. He curled his arms around Sarah's waist, drawing her in close and tilting his head to move in for another kiss. He leaned into the kiss, his mouth slightly parted as Sarah tickled his tongue with hers. A large, rough palm brought Sarah's head in closer, fingers gently caressing her dyed black locks. Sarah dragged her nails over his chiseled jaw, leaving red, bleeding scratches in their wake. With her fingers still tightly gripping Luke's shaggy hair, she tore his head away from hers. Her hand fingers let go of his hair and slid down his chest to his black silk tie. She tightened her hand around his tie and dragged him towards her bedroom, a coy smile dancing on her lips. Sarah twirled Luke around and pushed him down onto the bed, the mattress and bed frame creaking with his weight. Sarah cast his blazer off her shoulders and climbed up onto the bed. She lifted her knee and over Luke so that she was straddling his hips. She unraveled his tie and tugged it free of his shirt collar.

"Sarah-"

"Just be quiet, Agent Morrison." She stuffed his tie into his gaping maw and reached around his belt for his handcuffs. Sarah bit her lip seductively as she fastened the cold metal around one of his wrists, hooking them around a metal spoke in her head board and clicking the other around his other wrist so that his wrists were held above his head. Sarah leaned down and kissed down Luke's face and neck, her fingers unfastening his buttons and opening his shirt to reveal his toned torso. Luke's moans were lost in the fabric of his tie. Sarah continued to kiss down over his collarbone to his nipple. She bit down on his nipple, making him grunt in surprise and pain.

"Oh, Agent. You have no idea what I'm about to do to you." Luke's eyes widened as he lifted his head as far as he was able to see Sarah reaching for his belt and unbuckling it.

Luke was the first to awaken the following morning by the sound of his phone ringing. His face and chest were stinging, yet he was not entirely sure how. He went to reach for his phone to find that his wrists were still chained above his head. Sarah was curled up next to him, her head resting on his chest. Her back gently rose and fell as she slept, her hand pressed against the center of his abdomen. Each exhale danced coolly across his skin. The shrill ringing of his phone was relentless, piercing into his head. He tugged against the cuffs, hoping that the sound of scraping metal would wake Sarah. When it did not, Luke bucked his hips. The ringing was getting louder.

"Sarah? Sarah! I need to answer my phone." Sarah stirred, her eyelids fluttering. She lifted her eyes up from his torso, to his face and his cuffed hands. Sarah pushed herself up to her hands and knees and reached up to free his wrists. Luke gasped as he brought his hands down, sensation and circulation returning to his fingertips. He quickly picked up his phone to answer it.

" SA Luke Morrison?"

"Sir, we've got a hit of a man presenting at the emergency room at St Andrew's Hospital with a probable GSW to his left shoulder," came a frantic voice. Luke glanced at Sarah who had sat up straight and was listening intently.

"I'll be right there."

"Sir, one more thing. I haven't been able to get hold of SSA Carver."

"Don't worry, I'll catch her up." Luke's cheeks flushed with embarrassment as he hung up the call and turned to look at Sarah, "I need to freshen up," said Luke quickly as he darted off the bed for the bathroom. Luke stared into his reflection in the bathroom mirror above the basin. Four crimson scratches tracked down over his jaw and neck. Teeth marks were embedded into the skin around his nipple. He glanced down at his wrists which had red rings around them. He swallowed thickly. Things had taken a turn that he had not anticipated, but he had to admit, he had wanted it so much. He turned on the hot water faucet and cupped his hands underneath the stream of water, then splashed it against his face. A bead of water rolled down his nose into the basin. He could hear Sarah clattering in the next room, undoubtedly changing her uncharacteristic clothing from the night before. Luke quickly dried his face with the towel on the rail, then buttoned up his shirt, tucking the tail into his trousers and buckling his belt. He ran his still damp hands through his hair to detangle his curls. When he exited the bathroom, Sarah was in the process of pulling on a pair of black dress trousers from her closet over her hips. She had changed into a purple v-neck top. Sarah's eyes fell upon the man in her bathroom doorway, the seductive glint still remaining. Once dressed, Sarah grabbed her credentials, ID lanyard and firearm.

"Let's get to the hospital and catch this son of a bitch," instructed Sarah firmly, hooking her firearm on her belt and her lanyard around her neck. Luke nodded and followed her.

Chapter Ten- Jekyll and Hyde

The journey to the hospital was merely fifteen minutes away, yet it felt more akin to fifteen years. The atmosphere was tense. Luke gripped the steering wheel as though his entire being depended on it. Sarah had her left arm crossed over her chest with her right elbow nestled on top. Her fingertips brushed back and forth across her bottom lip in thought. Her eyes were fixed to a spot on the dashboard. Luke swallowed hard as he glanced sideways at Sarah. His skin stung mercilessly from sweat trickling down the side of his face and entering the gauges tracking over his jaw. The morning sun was much more intense than usual. Sarah's fingers inched up her face and she gingerly massaged her temple. Luke raised his eyebrows.

"You okay?" asked Luke softly, eyes darting between the superior agent and the road ahead. Sarah gave out a frustrated groan and Luke immediately knew that she had not slept after their night of heated passion and was experiencing the beginnings of an intense migraine. Sarah squinted against the flickering of the sunlight as they passed a series of trees and cupped her hand around her eyes to shield them.

"You have a migraine starting, don't you?"

"Mmhm," mumbled Sarah, her head slowly lowering and her hand cradling the back of her neck. Sweat beaded under the pads of her fingers. A wave of nausea swept through every fiber of Sarah's being. Her arm curled tighter around her waist as though she were trying to keep her internal organs within the confines of her abdomen. Luke quickly glanced at the visibly paling agent and pulled into an opening at the side of the road. He put the car into park and shifted in his seat so that he was facing Sarah. Cautiously, he reached forward, taking care not to startle her. His palm came to rest over the top of Sarah's clammy hand on her neck. Sarah let out a shaky breath. Stars and nebulas appeared before Sarah's eyes as she lowered her head further until it was between her parted knees.

"Sarah?"

"-m gonna.... Pass... Out..." pressed out Sarah, speech slurring. Luke felt Sarah's head fall limp under his palm. Her hand slid from her neck and landed on the seat with a gentle thud. Feeling somewhat helpless, Luke gently massaged the back of her neck.

"It's okay, Sarah. I'm right here." Luke turned up the air conditioning in the vehicle in a bid to cool the unconscious woman beside him. A small groan sounded as Sarah started to come to. She struggled slightly to sit herself up. Luke slid his hand down to the top of her back and grasped her upper arm with the other to ease her upright. Sarah's breaths were ragged as she stared straight ahead. Suddenly aware that someone had a tight hold on her arm, Sarah snapped her head sideways and narrowed her eyes at the offending appendage. Realizing Sarah's demeanor had changed, Luke removed his hands and held them up in surrender. His mouth bobbed in silent protest as Sarah's green gaze moved up to his face. The look in her eyes was unsettling, then changed again as her features softened. She eyed the scratches down Luke's jaw and reached forward a shaking hand towards them. Luke drew back slightly, unnerved by the Jekyll and Hyde change.

"Do they hurt?" asked Sarah, tracing her fingertips over the tender skin. Luke was unable to hold back a wince. Luke pressed himself back into the door as far as he could within the restraint of his seat belt.

"Uh... A little... I mean..." Luke found himself lost for words. A coy smile danced on Sarah's lips as she pressed a finger to his quivering lips to silence him. A burning rushed through his loins. Sarah unclipped her seatbelt and shuffled closer to him. She traced the tip of her tongue seductively over her bottom lip. Luke had nowhere to go and the seatbelt keeping him in his seat was cutting into his skin. Sarah gripped his shirt in her balled fists and pulled herself towards him. Luke's Adam's apple bobbed as he swallowed hard.

"Sarah? Please..." pressed out Luke, his voice cracking with anxiety. Sarah planted her lips hard on his, then released him. She slid back into her seat and fastened her seatbelt. With a trembling hand, Luke used the steering wheel to seat himself comfortably.

St Andrew's Hospital was quieter than one would expect. Perhaps it was the time of day. The doors to the emergency department slid open, allowing a rectangle of sunlight to glisten against the gray tiled floor. Sarah stepped through the doors first, her booted steps echoing in the unusually quiet waiting room. She walked with an air of command about her. She held her chin parallel to the ground, shoulders tense. Her right hand rested on the hilt of her glock. Sarah stopped and peered around at the waiting room. An older man cradled an injured hand into his chest, blood soaking through the checkered dish cloth that was wrapped tightly around it. A woman bounced her child on her knee. Sarah straightened her mouth into a grim line as her eyes fell upon the reception desk. She started towards the desk, eyes unblinking. Luke paused. The way in which Sarah could change was unnerving, and yet he found it attractive. He watched as her hips swayed with each step. She held an aura of authority. With a gulp, Luke followed her. Sarah tugged her credentials out of her pocket and opened them before the blonde woman seated behind the desk.

"SSA Sarah Carver. This is Special Agent Luke Morrison. We're from the Brooklyn FBI field office. We understand a man presented here with a GSW to the shoulder. He has dark hair, blue eyes and a scar over his left eye." The receptionist's mouth bobbed at the demeanor of the woman before her.

"I'm afraid that's confidential information. I need to know the reason why you need to know." Sarah leaned over the desk and narrowed her eyes.

"First of all, *miss*, I'm an FBI agent and this man is a suspect in a serial homicide case. Secondly, I'm the one that gave him that GSW." The receptionist gulped in fear. She quickly turned to her computer and typed rapidly on her keyboard, her nails tapping against the keys.

"H-his name is Nigel Carter. He was discharged an hour ago."

"His address. Now," growled Sarah.

"556 Rossworth Way, Brooklyn." Luke mouthed a silent apology at the visibly shaken receptionist as Sarah barged past him and made for the exit. Luke jogged behind her, his curls bouncing against his collar.

"Sarah? Sarah! Wait up!" Sarah whirled around and glared at him. Luke leaned against his knees as he tried to catch his breath. The sun bleached down on the pair as they stood, eyes fixed in a battle of wills. Sarah folded her arms over her chest and tapped her foot in annoyance.

"What the fuck was that, Sarah? The poor woman nearly pissed herself!" asked Luke as he pointed angrily at the hospital entrance. Sarah stepped up closer to him.

"We were too fucking late!"

"We got the address! Jesus, Sarah." Luke rested his left hand on his hip and brushed his hair out of his face. Several faces looked at the bickering pair as they passed. Sarah glared at him again, fury flashing in her eyes.

"Don't question me again."

"What? Sarah, there's ways and means of getting the information that we need, and that wasn't one of them. You're just bitter about the fact that he bested the great Sarah Carver." Instantly, Luke knew he had crossed a line. Sarah crackled with fury as she grabbed his tie and pulled him in close.

"How fucking dare you," pressed out Sarah, her voice low and dangerous. Luke's words were lost in his throat.

"I'm sorry," he croaked, his collar and tie tightening around his neck. Luke coughed dryly as Sarah released him from her deathly grip.

The car ride to the suspect's address was stifling and uncomfortable. Neither Sarah nor Luke spoke two words throughout the journey. Luke could sense that Sarah was still simmering under the surface. She was deathly silent. She clutched her firearm in her sweaty palm. Luke spotted an opening behind a red Chevrolet sedan and pulled into it. He barely had the engine turned off before Sarah flung the passenger door open. Luke let out a long, deflated sigh as he closed his eyes and rested the back of his head against the headrest of the seat that he occupied. Sarah already had the trunk of the car open and slid a Kevlar vest over her head. Sarah was a vessel of boiling rage. Her hands trembled with anger as she stretched the hook and loop straps over her shoulders and firmly pressed them down against the vest. She pulled the straps taut around her waist and secured them. The vest felt bone-crushing against her ribs. Luke slowly and cautiously approached, taking care not to startle his already unstable and explosive superior. Sarah had begun unloading and reloading her firearm when Luke strapped on his own Kevlar vest and haphazardly rolled his shirt sleeves to his elbows. Sarah stilled, aware that a shadow was looming over her. Luke fastened the last strap on his vest and pursed his lips as he stared at Sarah. For all Sarah's rapidly changing mood was somewhat terrifying, Luke found it extremely attractive. He took a moment as he lapped up Sarah's appearance. The Kevlar pinched her waist in, enhancing the curves of her hips. She had attempted to pull her hair back into a loose ponytail. A few strands of hair fell out of the hair band and over her face. Sarah still looked incredibly gaunt. Luke realized that he would have to force the stubborn woman back to the hospital once the case was solved. Luke withdrew his own firearm from his left hip and clicked off the safety. He raised his eyebrows and swallowed hard.

"You ready?" asked Luke anxiously. Sarah set her jaw and lifted her eyes from her glock up to Luke's face. Sweat beaded his forehead. The skin surrounding the scratches over his was reddened, eliciting a pit of regret to form in the pits of Sarah's stomach. Sarah nodded, the loose strands of hair over her face swaying.

Luke was the first to approach the property, defensively keeping Sarah behind him. The area was rough and dilapidated. Luke crept towards the front door. Dark green paint was peeling from rotting wood. The door frame was partially hanging off blackened brick work. Luke took in a deep breath and pressed the palm of his left hand against the door to test it, his gun clasped in his right hand. The door opened under Luke's touch. He transferred his firearm back to his left hand and used his right to steady his wrist. Sarah was very close. He could feel her hot breath against his back.

"Hello? This is the FBI. We're coming in," shouted Luke, his voice echoing throughout the empty hallway. Sarah stepped around him, her own firearm raised in front of her. She gestured to Luke to take the left side towards the kitchen. Luke nodded in a silent, mutual understanding and disappeared into the darkness. Sarah slowly made her way up the stairs, her green eyes darting in every direction. Her heart pounded a hole in her ribs. Dust fell around her, highlighted by the light filtering through the dirty window at the top of the stairs. Sarah stepped up onto the landing, her back pressed against the peeling wallpaper. She felt her lungs constrict with fear. The dust swirling around her and the musky smell was stifling. Sarah edged along a small landing where there were three doors. She clasped her fingers around the doorknob of the first door. It swung open to an entirely empty room; no bed, no carpets, no furniture. The anxiety crept its way through every fiber of Sarah's being as she crept towards the second door. As she approached the second door and reached out for the doorknob, a sound pricked at her senses from behind. Her firearm shot up as she peered around. Realizing that she was alone, Sarah turned back to the door. As she reached for it a second time, she felt an arm around her throat and pulled her back towards the third bedroom.

Chapter Eleven- Face to Face With Hell

Sarah fought with all of her might against the strong arm that was obscuring her breathing. She twisted her hips to both sides as she tried to wriggle out of the grip. Her mouth bobbed as she desperately tried to regain her breathing. She concentrated hard as her feet slipped against the floor. She felt her whole body sail through the air as she was thrown into the room. Her right shoulder crashed against the floor, followed closely by her head. Stars danced in front of Sarah's eyes as she tried to push herself up from the floor. Her fingers numbly scrambled for her gun that had skidded a short distance away from her. Nigel Carter towered over the top of her. Sarah looked up with bleary eyes. Nigel delivered a harsh kick to Sarah's abdomen. She coughed as she tried to regain her breath. Nigel brought his boot down hard on her fingers, the audible sound of bones cracking beneath his sole. Sarah gritted her teeth, determined that she would show the monster no weakness. Luke's voice sounded, followed by footsteps.

"Sarah? Sarah? Everything okay?" Nigel menacingly hovered his boot over her battered hand in a stark warning. He reached down for Sarah's gun and took it into his hands.

"In here! Third bedroom!" yelled Sarah. Nigel whirled around and struck her in the face with the butt of the gun, splitting her pale cheek. She gasped, blood trickling down her face. Luke's footsteps quickened. Nigel turned towards the door, raised the gun and fired. Sarah was seeing double, but she was certain she saw Luke's figure crumple to the ground. Luke had indeed fallen. He clutched his left shoulder where the bullet had just missed his vest. Crimson liquid blossomed across his shirt. Nigel had two experienced agents in his claws. Luke raised his gun in his trembling, non-dominant hand and fired back. Nigel's left leg disappeared underneath him as the bullet tore through his thigh. He dropped to the ground with a heavy thud. Dust and dirt clouded around him. Sarah managed to ease herself up to unsteady feet and stumbled towards the heap of a moaning man on the ground. She retrieved her firearm and pointed it at him. She had not anticipated that he would have a knife on him. A flash of a blade appeared before the blade was plunged deep into her foot. She groaned in pain and fired involuntarily in reflex. Nigel stilled, eyes wide and unblinking, a neat hole in his forehead. With the knife still protruding out of the top of her foot, Sarah stepped over the man in front of her and used the walls to guide herself towards Luke who lay on the ground, his teeth gritted in agony. Blood spilled between his fingers. Sarah dropped heavily to her knees. She ignored the sharp pinch of the knife being jostled in her foot and pressed a hand to Luke's shoulder. Luke's eyes sprung open and stared directly into Sarah's. Sarah spoke quickly into the microphone clipped to her vest.

"This is SSA Carver. I need medics at 556 Rossworth Way. Agent down. I repeat, agent down." Luke gave a smile, pained smile.

"Better make that two." Luke had noticed that Sarah's eyes were unfocussed and her skin had turned a sickly shade of gray. The fingers on her right hand has turned an alarming shade of black, blue and purple. Sarah's eyes rolled back into her head as she slumped over onto Luke, her hand still pressed against his wound.

A blinding white light was the first thing that Sarah saw as she peeled her eyes open. She questioned whether or not this was the white light many associated with death. Though, as her vision came back into focus, this was not the case. Blurry at first, Sarah came to realize that she was in the back of an ambulance. Her body jostled on the gurney periodically as the vehicle made turns or hit bumps in the road. A face loomed over hers, shining a pen torch in her eyes. Sarah groaned at the agony piercing through her skull.

"Agent Carver? I'm Susie. You're in safe hands now." Sarah reached up and pulled the oxygen mask down from over her face.

"What happened?" asked Sarah groggily.

"You have a mild concussion. I suspect you have some broken fingers and a broken rib. We'll get the knife removed at the hospital."

"Luke? Where is he? Is he okay?" Susie reached over and placed the mask back over her patient's face.

"He's on the other bus. I won't know until we're at the hospital." Realizing that she was not going to get any information, Sarah succumbed to the tiredness that was spreading throughout every fiber of her being.

Sarah grew increasingly frustrated with each passing hour in the hospital. Bandages had been wrapped into a bizarre linen boot around the protruding weapon in her foot. She had been poked and prodded from several different professionals and it had started to test her patience. A large bruise had formed on her forehead above her eyebrow from the collision with the wooden floor. A dressing had been taped over the neatly stitched wound on her cheek which partially obscured her vision. Her second and third fingers on her right hand had been strapped together with medical tape, a soft piece of gauze providing cushioning between the two heavily bruised appendages. She had heard nothing about Luke which caused her a great deal of anxiety. A male nurse drew back the blue curtain around the bed that Sarah occupied and picked up the clipboard from the foot of the bed. Sarah narrowed her eyes at the unsuspecting man and curled the fingers of her left hand into a fist.

"What is going on?" asked Sarah through clenched teeth. The nurse raised an eyebrow as he lifted his head to look at her.

"Excuse me?"

"I've been here for hours. I have a knife in my foot, no one is telling me what is going on and I have no idea how my partner is! Why won't any of you tell me a damned thing?"

"The doctor will be here shortly to discuss the findings of your scans. I have no information about your partner."

"Well, here's an idea for you, *genius,* go and find me some information, or even someone with enough of a brain cell to actually help me!"

"Ms Carver-"

"*Agent* Carver."

"Agent Carver." Sarah snapped her head up at a stern-looking, older man who had silently sidled up beside the nurse. He had a gray mustache and short cropped hair, reminding Sarah of an army drill sergeant. He wore dark green scrubs under a pristine white coat. A pair of round, wire spectacles balanced on his bulbous nose, "I am Doctor Matfen. Making a fuss in my ER, I see?" Sarah scowled at him, a snarl tugging at the corner of her mouth.

"Don't you dare-" growled Sarah in a low, dangerous voice.

"Be quiet, agent, and listen. You have a mild concussion so you will experience some intense headaches for a while-"

"More intense than the migraines? Jesus. Don't patronize me."

"Yes, yes. Your CT scan shows a lesion in the temporal lobe of your brain. Your migraines will increase in intensity until the concussion resolves. Neurologists are going to meet with you to discuss your options. You have broken your middle and ring proximal phalanges. You have also fractured your sixth rib on the left. We don't need to give you any further treatment for those. As for the knife, it has missed the major structures of the foot so we can go ahead and remove it. Any questions?" Sarah stared at her blanket in disbelief, as if her entire world had flipped upside down, "Agent Carver? Do you have any questions?"

"How is Luke?" pressed out Sarah, her voice strained with emotion.

"Luke?" asked Doctor Matfen.

"My partner. Luke Morrison. He was shot. I need to know if he's okay." Doctor Matfen cleared his throat.

"Agent Morrison is fine. He may have some trouble with his fine motor skills for now in that hand but I'm confident that he'll recover with physical therapy." Sarah lay back into her pillows and sighed.

"I have to see him. Please." Sarah hated herself for begging, and for the show of weakness in her voice. Doctor Matfen nodded to the nurse who silently slipped out of the cubicle.

"We'll see how he is feeling. In the meantime, we need to get this knife out of your foot."

"Doctor?" Sarah's voice was small and child-like, a startling contrast to a few moments prior. Doctor Matfen's face softened.

"Yes?"

"In your professional opinion... This lesion... Is it... That?" Doctor Matfen gave out a long solemn sigh.

"Most likely. The neurologist will review your CT scan and your previous MRI. I'm afraid it's not in my remit to run through options and prognoses with you." Sarah nodded sadly, her eyes fixed on her hands folded on her lap. The last time Sarah felt so lost, she was receiving that dreaded call from the local police.

"Sarah Carver?" came the raspy voice of a police officer.

"Speaking."

"My name is Officer Eckhart of the Brooklyn Police Department. I'm calling in relation to Danny Fairfax." Sarah straightened in her swivel chair.

"What happened?"

"There has been an RTA at the junction of 1st and 22nd. A blue sedan has collided with Mr Fairfax's car at high speed. I'm afraid he was DOA." Sarah's hands trembled, tears threatening her lower lashes.

"DOA?"

"Afraid so, ma'am. The other driver was also DOA. There were empty vodka bottles in the foot well of the vehicle. We're waiting for tox but we suspect that the driver was under the influence. I'm very sorry for your loss. Could you come to the ME office so that we can make formal identification?"

"Sure." Sarah promptly hung up the call. She stared at the bouquet of lilies that rested on her desk. He had only been gone a matter of minutes. Six minutes was all it took for his life to be ripped away from him. Sarah's heart shattered into a million pieces in that single moment.

Chapter Twelve- Aftermath

Sarah found herself lost in a swirling vortex of thoughts, falling deeper and deeper into her own subconscious. Her thoughts raced, yet moved in slow motion. She stared blankly at the small patch of blood soaking through the bandage wound tightly around her foot. The room blurred around her. It was as though she was trapped in a stop motion animated movie. She desperately wanted the previous few hours to be a nightmare. She hoped that she would awake and find herself in her bed having had a vivid nightmare. She curled her toes and felt the pinch of pain as her inflamed tendons tightened. This was far from being a vivid nightmare. Sarah glanced up at the sound of shuffling, her dyed black locks dangling around her face and falling into the collar of her hospital gown. Her eyes trailed up the bare legs, past the hospital gown, the arm encased in a large blue sling that was wrapped around a neck to the worn out face of Luke. He smiled at her, his eyes heavy with pain and exhaustion.

"I hear you're making quite the commotion?" Sarah's eyebrows shot up and threw back her blankets. Ignoring the sharp pain in her foot, she wrapped her arms around Luke's neck, forcing him to bend down slightly, "Okay... What's that for?"

"Thank God you're okay! I was so worried when they wouldn't tell me anything!" responded Sarah, her voice muffled by the itchy gown covering Luke's shoulder.

"I'm okay. The bullet nicked some tendons but nothing major. I'll live." Luke drew back and stared into Sarah's pools of green. There was something there. A new pain, "Sarah? Something's wrong. Talk to me." Sarah looked down to the floor and let her arms drop by her sides. She rested her buttocks against the edge of the bed and pushed herself up onto it so that her legs dangled over the side. Luke perched next to her, his eyes never leaving her bruised face.

"They did a CT scan. I have a concussion. That's not all. They found a lesion in my temporal lobe." Sarah felt her throat closing up and her eyes stung with unshed tears. Luke frowned.

"A lesion? What, like a tumor or something?" Sarah nodded sadly, her head bowed.

"A neurologist is reviewing my scans but they suspect it's cancerous." Luke's mouth dropped open in a silent 'O'.

"What are they going to do? I mean, there has to be something?"

"I won't know until they review the scans. Luke?" Sarah lifted her chin to face the man seated beside her, silent tears tracking over her cheeks, "I'm scared." Luke curled his uninjured arm around Sarah's shoulders and drew her in close. He rested his chin on top of her head.

"It'll be okay. You'll get through this. *We'll* get through this." Luke ran his fingers through Sarah's hair. Sarah wrapped her arms around his waist as though he were her life force and she would die if he let go. Luke had already begun going through plans A-Z in his head. As exhausted as the pair was, Sarah found safety and solace in the other agent.

Sarah was grateful to return to her apartment. She had been ordered to rest and meet with the neurologist in two weeks to go over her scans and treatment options. Her crutches clicked against the wooden floor as her apartment door swung open. Everything was exactly as she had left it. She caught the scent of Luke's cologne. In the heat of the day, she had forgotten their night of passion the previous night. Sarah tugged the duffel bag over her head and slung it to the floor with a thud. She did not care about changing into her pyjamas. She just wanted to sleep. Lots of sleep. Sarah shuffled her way to her bedroom. The bed sheets were still twisted from the night before. A pair of handcuffs dangled from the head board. Sarah felt her cheeks flush. With a sigh, she dropped heavily onto the side of the bed and lay her crutches on the floor next to the bed. She eyed the glass of whiskey that had stood stagnant for days. The caramel coloured liquid still looked exactly as it had. Sarah threw open her drawer and took the strip of Tylenol. She was down to her last two pills. She popped them out into her palm and tipped them into her mouth. Grabbing the glass, Sarah gulped the remaining beverage to flush the tablets down. She grimaced at the taste and the burn of the alcohol as it slid down her throat. Sarah lay back into her pillows and lifted her aching legs onto the bed. Sleep took her quicker than she had anticipated.

Luke lay awake in his bed, staring blankly at the ceiling. His brain felt jumbled with the thoughts swirling around. He was deeply concerned for Sarah, yet he had the confidence that she would be alright. Sarah was exceptionally stubborn and hard-headed, so she would not be beaten by whatever the lesion was. He also had a deep affection for his superior that extended far beyond professional respect. She gave him a thrill that sent tidal waves throughout his stomach. She was beautiful, intelligent and humorous. He felt conflicted. She was still grieving for her fiancé. Luke groaned, his head pounding with the cacophony of thoughts battering his mind. His shoulder throbbed with each beat of his heart. Realizing that sleep would continue to evade him, Luke threw back the covers and swung his legs over the side of the bed. His bare back bristled with the cool air creeping in through his open bedroom window. He gently traced his fingertips over the dressing taped over the wound in his shoulder. He bowed his head, his shaggy hair falling about his face. The case had sapped every ounce of his energy. He sighed and dragged himself to his feet. He padded his way to the lounge, his bare feet sticking to the hardwood floor. His lounge was warm and comfortable, giving off ancient library vibes with the brown leather furniture and bookcases filled with old, yet well kept books. A gentle glow of moonlight was cast in a circle across the floor from the large window overlooking the street below.

Luke cradled his aching shoulder as he made his way into the kitchen that was bathed in darkness. He gave the light switch a quick flick, filling the small, yet tidy kitchen with warm light. He pursed his lips as he tapped the button on the coffee machine, the sweet symphony of the thick brown liquid bubbling and hissing as it heated up. With his unhindered arm, Luke reached up to the wooden cupboard above him and slowly pulled the door open. His crockery collection was sparse, given that he lived alone and had spent much of his adult life alone. His job meant he had no time for relationships. He was happy with his coffee and his books, though he was unable to help feeling that something was missing. He shook his head to rid himself of his thoughts, his hair swaying and brushing against the nape of his neck. He selected a ceramic mug with the chemical symbol for caffeine printed on it. He poured the steaming hot coffee into his mug and added a heap of sugar to the mixture. He carried the mug back to the lounge and lowered himself carefully into the sofa. A book lay unread on the coffee table. Luke gave a small smile to himself as he reached for the book.

It was as though Sarah had turned into a grizzly bear with a sore head on awakening. For all her slumber had not been disturbed by her phone ringing, the pain that shot through her foot had kept her awake for much of the night. She stormed about her apartment without the aid of her crutches, purely out of frustration. Clothes were scattered across her bedroom floor and dirty crockery filled the sink in the kitchen. Her arms were filled with clean laundry as she returned to her bedroom to make an effort to fold them and put them away. A knock sounded at the door. She snapped her head sideways at the offending noise.

"Go away!" she yelled at no one in particular. The knock sounded again, "I said, get lost!" The third knock echoed throughout the empty apartment. Sarah groaned outwardly and dropped the pile of laundry on her bed. She limped back to the front door and threw it open, "What?" she snapped. Sarah's eyes fell upon a pair of jean-clad legs, her mouth hanging open in surprise. As she inspected the figure at the door, the heavy metal shirt and black leather biker jacket, she realized then that she had never seen Luke in anything other than a button down shirt and dress trousers. His left arm was encased in the sling. His eyebrows were raised at her.

"Luke? What are you doing here?"

"I need to talk to you." Sarah noticed that the man looked exceptionally tired, the dark circles even darker around his eyes. Sarah stepped back to allow him in. Luke glanced around uncomfortably.

"Can I get you some coffee?" asked Sarah, her voice tinged with concern.

"Please." Luke seated himself on the sofa and looked down at the floor. He fiddled anxiously with the sling supporting his arm. He could hear the hissing of the coffee machine and clanking of mugs from the kitchen, "Do you need any help?" Sarah gave muffled curses as she tried to carry out a simple task. Luke eased himself back to his feet and made his way to the kitchen. Sarah was clinging to the counter and her foot raised to relieve the pressure, "Are you okay?" Sarah glanced over her shoulder.

"Yeah. I'm good. What do you want to talk about?"

"Wouldn't you rather wait until you're sat down?"

"Luke, you know I'm impatient. Just spit it out already." Luke pursed his lips and leaned his back against the counter.

"Sarah? I know you're my boss and FBI agents shouldn't enter into personal relationships... Jesus, I don't know how to say this... God, I suck!" Luke pressed a palm to his forehead in frustration as he paced the kitchen floor. A hand came to rest on his arm, halting him in his tracks, "I know you're still grieving for Danny, and I get it. Really I do. But I can't help feeling the way I do."

"It's okay. Just say it."

"I'm attracted to you. You ignite something inside of me that I never knew existed-"

"Shut up, Agent Morrison and just kiss me." Sarah shoved him back against the counter, his spine colliding with the edge. She tightly gripped the nape of his neck and forced his head down to meet hers. Luke had a look of uncertainty on his face that was quickly replaced by one of determination. He tugged his arm out of the sling and gently cupped Sarah's face with his rough palms. He planted his lips firmly on hers, his hair tickling her face. Sarah's mouth willingly opened up, allowing Luke's tongue to dance on hers. Luke's fingers entwined in Sarah's loose waves.

Sarah limped her way to the bedroom with a fistful of Luke's shirt as she dragged him with her. She gave him a hard shove onto the bed amongst the clean laundry. Luke wasted no time in ignoring the fire rippling through his shoulder as he relieved himself of his jacket and shirt, revealing his surprisingly toned abdomen. Sarah clambered on top of him, peeling her strapped vest top off over her head. She fumbled with his belt and dragged his jeans down over his hips. Their mouths smashed against one another in their fit of passion. Luke ran his hands up and down Sarah's torso, absorbing the softness of her skin. Sarah tightly gripped his hair and wrenched his head away. She kissed roughly down his neck to the dressing on his shoulder. Luke gave an equally aroused and pained groan. Sarah slapped a palm over his mouth, her fingertips pressing into his cheeks.

"Shhh and let me enjoy this." Sarah licked his earlobe then bit down hard. Luke's yelp was muffled by the hand. Her hand slid down and came to rest over his throat, "You're under arrest, Agent Morrison," whispered Sarah seductively as she eyed the handcuffs on her headboard.

"Oh, yeah? Are you going to cuff me and do bad things to me?"

"Oh, you bet your sweet ass." A smile danced on Luke's lips as he shuffled back on the bed. Sarah forced Luke's right arm up and clicked one of the cuffs firmly around his wrist. Luke's shoulder pinched as his left arm was wrenched above his head and cuffed next to his other wrist. He lifted his head to see Sarah wrestling his jeans and underwear down over the rest of his legs, leaving him stark naked on the bed. Her eyes wandered hungrily over his body and the large pink scars that criss-crossed over his outer thighs. Sarah slid off the bed.

"Where are you going?" Sarah kissed her teeth as she left the room, her hips swaying. Luke could feel his groins burning with lust. Sarah returned with a roll of shiny gray duct tape in her hands, "What's this?"

"You have been a very bad boy, agent. You need to be punished." Sarah grasped Luke's ankles and tied them to the bottom of the bed frame so that he legs were spread apart. She climbed back onto the bed and crawled up to him. She peeled another strip away from the roll and held it taut, "And you're going to take your punishment quietly." Luke nodded as the tape was torn from the roll and smoothed it over his lips. Sarah leaned into him, her breasts pressed into his bare chest. She kissed him firmly on his taped mouth and wiggled herself out of her shorts and underwear. She lowered herself onto his hips, eliciting a muffled groan from the prone man on the bed. Luke pulled against his restraints as Sarah moved expertly on him. His cheeks flushed with lust, his moans of pleasure lost into the tape. He thrust his head back into the pillow, his sharp jaw tilted into the air, exposing the veins in his neck. Faint pink lines remained over Luke's jaw. Sarah traced her fingertips over the tape and down his chin, tugging his head down so that he could see her. She gave a gasp as she climaxed. She fell to the side of Luke, panting heavily. Luke's chest rose and fell rapidly as he breathed through his nose.

"You need to remain in custody for a little while, Agent Morrison. I'm not quite done punishing you-" The shrill sound of a phone ringing interrupted the pair. Sarah closed her eyes, wishing that she had entered another dimension. Luke gave another muffled moan of exasperation. Sarah quickly shut off her cell phone and slid herself over Luke, "Where were we?"

End

Printed in Great Britain
by Amazon